Master Bible Quiz
Volume - 1

Master Bible Quiz
Volume - 1

Ashish Philip

2016

Master Bible Quiz (Volume–1) — published by the Rev. Dr. Ashish Amos of the Indian Society for Promoting Christian Knowledge (ISPCK), Post Box 1585, Kashmere Gate, Delhi-110006.

ISBN: 978-81-8465-552-0

Laser typeset by

ISPCK, Post Box 1585, 1654, Madarsa Road, Kashmere Gate, Delhi-110006 • *Tel:* 23866323

e-mail: ashish@ispck.org.in • ella@ispck.org.in
website: www.ispck.org.in

Contents

Answers

Contents

Preface

Making a decision was only the beginning of things. When someone makes a decision, he is really diving into a strong current that will carry him into places he had never dreamed of when he first made the decision.

The Alchemist, Paulo Coelho

Truly, decision making is only the beginning of a new set of events. Sometimes many forces act together in this decision making and work together to give a direction.

Initially 'The Master Bible Quiz' book was compiled for my personal use and it was not intended to be published. Later when I showed this compilation to some priests and to our Bishop, they all encouraged me to get it published.

Since, this book was for my personal use, the language is very simple. It can be used by people of any age, Bible experts or otherwise. The answers along with references are mentioned in the book.

Preface

This first volume is the first in a series of 9 volumes of 'The Master Bible Quiz book.' The first volume is a compilation of 1400 questions and answers from the Pentateuch i.e. first five books of the Old Testament, from Genesis to Deuteronomy.

I was inspired by my parents, Church, Sunday School and Youth league to write this book. As regular quiz competitions are conducted in our church, I started preparing the questions from various books of the Bible. It eventually took the form of a quiz book.

Though it took me about a year to prepare this book, the effort started a long time ago.

The sole aim behind publishing this book is for the benefit of children and youths or anyone interested in Bible Quiz competitions. This book will help them to not only prepare for such competitions in an effortless manner but also help them to understand the scripture.

I sincerely thank all those who encouraged and guided me to get this book published. My sincere thanks and gratitude to all the Achens, Brothers of Leonard Theological College, Mrs. Letty Mathew M, my parents, my wife, my son Adriel, and all those who supported and prayed for me.

Genesis

Genesis

The genre of Genesis is a Narrative History and Genealogies. It was written by Moses, at about 1400 B.C. Key personalities include Adam, Eve, Noah, Abraham, Sarah, Isaac, Rebekah, Jacob and Joseph. This book was written to record God's creation of the world and to demonstrate His love for all that He created.

Genesis is the first book of the Law and also the first book of the entire Bible. The name Genesis literally means *"In the Beginning"*. It explains the actual events of one of the most debated subjects of our current day... the origin of life. Genesis describes the Lord God, who is infinite and all-powerful, creating everything that exists, by the power of His spoken Word, out of nothing. He essentially creates material matter out of nonmaterial things.

- Chapters 1-11:28, Moses explains the creation of all things, *"In the beginning God created the heavens and the earth" (1:1)*. He quickly switches to the fall of humankind in sin and separation from God in chapter 3; then, how God implemented His judgement on the wicked earth. Through a universal flood and by selecting and sparing Noah, a faithful man, and his family, God wipes out humanity and starts again, with one secluded family.

- Chapters 11:28-36, God begins to carry out His plan of redemption in the beginning stages of establishing His own nation of Israel. It is through Abraham, again one faithful man, who God calls and promises to bless with a multitude of people and through them bless the entire world, *"... and in you all the families of the earth will be blessed" (12:3).*

- Chapters 37-50, God faithfully raises and protects the generations from Abraham as He had promised, all the way through unto Joseph while in Egypt. God blesses Abraham's son and his sons. Through their disappointments and failures, He displays His power and sovereignty in their lives; but at the end of the book of Genesis, God's people are in a foreign land and wondering about the Promised Land.

1. How many chapters are there in this book?

2. How many verses are there in this book?

3. Who is the author of this book?

4. When was this book written?

5. In the beginning when God created the universe how did the earth look like?

6. Where was the spirit of God moving?

7. What was the first creation of God?

8. What did God see as good in his creation for the first time?

9. What did God name light as?

10. What did God name darkness as?

11. What was the second creation of God?

12. What was the third creation of God?

13. What did God name land as?

14. What did God name the collection of water as?

15. On which day did God create the plants?

16. What was the fourth creation of God?

17. What did God make to rule over the day?

18. What did God make to rule over the night?

19. What was the fifth creation of God?

20. What did God command them to do?

21. What was the sixth creation of God?

22. How did human beings look like?

23. Who had the power over animals, birds and fishes?

24.   In how many days did God create the whole universe?

25.   For which two days of creation has it been mentioned, "God was pleased"?

26.   Which day was blessed and kept apart as a special day?

27.   In which side/direction did God plant the Garden of Eden?

28.   Which trees were planted in the middle of the Garden of Eden?

29.   What are the names of the rivers that flowed beyond the Garden of Eden?

30.   Which river flowed around the country of Havilah?

31.   In which country were pure gold, rare perfume and precious stones found?

32.   Which river flowed around the country of Cush?

33.   Which river flowed east of Assyria?

34.   The fruit of which tree did God forbid man to eat in the Garden of Eden?

35.   Who named all the birds and the animals?

36.   Name the first person who fell into a deep sleep.

37.   How did God make a woman?

38.   Which was the most cunning animal that the Lord God made?

39.   Who asked the first question in the Holy Bible?

40.   Who told the first lie in the Holy Bible?

41.   After disobeying, how did Adam and Eve cover themselves?

42.   Name the only animal which has been cursed by God.

43. What promise was made regarding the seed of the woman?

44. Who is the mother of all human beings?

45. Who did God place with a flaming sword on the east side of the Garden of Eden to keep anyone from coming near the tree of life?

46. Who was the first/born of Adam?

47. What was the job of Cain?

48. What was the job of Abel?

49. Who was the first person in the Holy Bible to become furious and who scowled in anger?

50. Who was the first murderer?

51. Who said, "Am I my brother's keeper?"

52. For whom was the first mark/sign given in the Holy Bible?

53. Where did Cain live after he went away from the Lord's presence?

54. Who was the first born son of Cain?

55. Who built a city and named it after his son and what was the name of the city?

56. Who was the first/born son of Enoch?

57. Name the first person in the Bible who had two wives.

58. What was the name of Lamech's wives?

59. Who was the ancestor of those who raise livestock and live in tents?

60. Who was the ancestor of all musicians who play the harp and the flute?

61. Who made all kinds of tools out of bronze and iron?

62. Who was the sister of Tubal Cain?

63. Who was the mother of Tubal Cain?

64. How many lives had to be taken to avenge Lamech?

65. Which son was born to replace Abel?

66. Who was the first born son of Seth?

67. In whose time did people begin using the Lord's holy name in worship?

68. What was the age of Adam when Seth was born?

69. How many years did Adam live after the birth of Seth?

70. At what age did Adam die?

71. What was the age of Seth when Enosh was born?

72. At what age did Seth die?

73. How old was Enosh when Kenan was born?

74. At what age did Enosh die?

75. What was the age of Kenan when Mahalalel was born?

76. At what age did Kenan die?

77. How old was Mahalalel when Jared was born?

78. At what age did Mahalalel die?

79. How old was Jared when Enoch was born?

80. At what age did Jared die?

81. How old was Enoch when Methuselah was born?

82. What unusual thing happened to Enoch?

83. What was the age of Enoch when God took him away?

84. What was the age of Methuselah when Lamech was born?

85. At what age did Methuselah die?

86. Which man lived the longest?

87. What was the age of Lamech when Noah was born?

88. At what age did Lamech die?

89. How old was Noah when he had sons?

90. What were the names of Noah's sons?

91. From whose time was the age of humankind reduced?

92. Who was the first man in the Bible with whom God was pleased?

93. Who was the only good man of his time and had no fault in him?

94. Out of which tree did God ask Noah to build the ark with?

95. What was coated inside and outside of the rooms of Noah's ark?

96. What was the dimension of Noah's ark?

97. How many doors were there in the Ark?

98. How many pairs of ritually clean animals did God ask Noah to take into the ark?

99. How many pairs of ritually unclean animals did God ask Noah to take into the ark?

100. How old was Noah when flood came on the earth?

101. For how many days after Noah and his family went into the boat was the earth flooded?

102. For how many days and nights did it rain during the flood at Noah's time?

103. Who closed the door of the ark?

104. How deep were the mountains covered under the flood?

105. For how many days did the water flood the earth?

106. On which mountain did Noah's ark come to rest?

107. When did the ark come to rest at Ararat Mountain?

108. When did the top of the mountains become visible?

109. Which bird did Noah send out of the ark first?

110. Which birds did Noah send out to see if the water had receded from the surface of the ground?

111. When did the water dry up from the earth?

112. Who built the first altar for the Lord?

113. In whose time did God allow humankind to eat animals?

114. What sign did God give to Noah to symbolize that he will never again destroy the earth by flood?

115. Who was the father of Canaan?

116. What was the job of Noah?

117. Who was the first person to plant a vineyard?

118. Who was the first person to get drunk in the Bible?

119. Name the person who drank wine and lay naked in his tent.

120. Name the sons of Noah who covered his nakedness.

121. Who is the first character in the Bible who received a father's curse?

122. Whom did Noah curse to be a slave to his brothers?

123. How many more years did Noah live after the flood?

124. What was the age of Noah when he died?

125. Who was the father of Nimrod?

126. Who was Nimrod?

127. Who became the first mighty warrior on the earth?

128. Which city is between Nineveh and Calah?

129. Name the first city which has been mentioned as "the great city" in the Bible.

130. In whose time was the earth divided?

131. Who was the brother of Peleg?

132. What was the name of the city where God confused languages?

133. Who was the first born son of Shem?

134. Who was the father of Terah?

135. How old was Nahor when Terah was born?

136. Who was the father of Abram?

137. What were the names of Abram's brother?

138. Name the son of Terah who died in his native place.

139. Who was the wife of Abram?

140. Who was the wife of Nahor?

141. Who was the daughter of Haran?

142. Who was the father of Lot?

143. Where did Terah die?

144. What was the age of Terah when he died?

145. With whom did God make his first promise, "I will give you many descendants and they will become a great nation"?

146.   How old was Abram when he started out from Haran?

147.   Where did God appear to Abram first?

148.   Name the person who built an altar at the place where God appeared to him.

149.   Name the Hebrew woman whom the Egyptians saw as beautiful.

150.   Because of whom did the Lord send terrible diseases to the Pharaoh and his people?

151.   Which woman was a prophet's wife and taken into the Pharaoh's palace?

152.   Name the cities which looked like the Garden of the Lord or like the land of Egypt before these cities were destroyed by the Lord.

153.   Who lived among the cities of the plain and pitched his tents near Sodom?

154.   The people of which city were wicked and sinned greatly against the Lord?

155.   Where did Abram live in Hebron?

156.   What was the other name of Zoar?

157.   In the olden days, what was there in place of the Dead Sea?

158.   What was the other name of Kadesh?

159.   According to the Bible, where did the first battle take place?

160.   How many kings took part in the first battle?

161.   Which valley was full of tar pits?

162.   Name the kings who fell into the tar pits.

163. Name the book where Abram has been termed as a Hebrew.

164. With how many trained men did Abram rescue Lot?

165. Which valley is also known as King's valley?

166. After the rescue of Lot, where did Abram meet the King of Sodom?

167. Who was the King of Salem and the priest of the Most High God?

168. Name the king who brought bread and wine for Abram.

169. To whom did Abram give a tenth of everything?

170. Name the person who gave the first tithe in the Bible.

171. To whom did Abram swear an oath with raised hand?

172. Name the men of Abram who received a share from King of Sodom.

173. Who was the slave of Abram?

174. Who fell into a deep sleep as the sun was setting?

175. For how many years did God say that the descendants of Abram will be enslaved and mistreated in a foreign country?

176. Which river of Egypt is also known as the great river?

177. Who inherited the land of Canaan at the time of Abram?

178. Who is the first known barren woman in the Bible?

179. Who was the Egyptian slave-girl of Sarai?

180. Name the woman who was pregnant and started despising her mistress.

181. Which slave ran away when her mistress treated her cruelly?

182. Where did the angel of the Lord meet Hagar when she ran away from her mistress?

183. Who lived like a wild donkey?

184. Who did the angel of the Lord say would live apart from all his relatives?

185. What is the well between Kadesh and Bered known as?

186. How old was Abram when Ishmael was born?

187. How old was Abram when God appeared to him and changed his name?

188. Who became the father of many nations?

189. As a sign of the Covenant, what did the Lord ask Abraham to do?

190. How many days after birth does a male child have to be circumcised?

191. Who became the mother of many nations?

192. For whom did God promise, "He will be the father of twelve rulers"?

193. How old was Abraham when he was circumcised?

194. How old was Ishmael when he was circumcised?

195. What were the names of the father and son who had been circumcised on the same day as commanded by the Lord?

196. Name the person who welcomed and greeted his guests under a tree.

197. Name the woman who laughed after hearing the promise from the Lord.

198. Who denied that she wasn't laughing because she was afraid?

199. Who asked the Lord, "Are you really going to destroy the innocent with the guilty"?

200. Who called himself as dust and ashes?

201. How many times did Abraham plead for Sodom and Gomorrah?

202. For how many innocent people in the city did Abraham ask God to forgive the people of Sodom and Gomorrah six times?

203. Where was Lot sitting when the angels came to Sodom?

204. Who were strongly insisted by Lot to come to his house and be his guests?

205. Who is mentioned as the first person who baked bread without yeast?

206. Whose house was surrounded at night by young and old men of Sodom?

207. All the men of which city were struck with blindness?

208. Where did Lot reach when the sun was rising?

209. What did the Lord rain on Sodom and Gomorrah to destroy it?

210. Name the Bible character who was turned into a pillar of salt.

211. Who were the women who lived in a cave?

212. Who were the daughters who made their own father drunk?

213. Who became pregnant by her father?

214. Who is the father of Moabites?

215. Who is the father of Ammonites?

216. Who was the king of Gerar whom the Lord appear to?

217. Who said, "Lord will you destroy an innocent nation"?

218. Name the person whose step-sister was his wife.

219. Which king of Gerar gave Abraham sheep, cattle and male and female slaves?

220. How many silver shekels were given by Abimelech to Abraham to prove Sarah's innocence?

221. Because of whom did the Lord make it impossible for any woman in Abimelech's palace to have children?

222. Which prophet prayed for King Abimelech and his people?

223. What was the age of Abraham when Isaac was born?

224. Who said, "God has brought me laughter, and everyone who hears about this will laugh with me."?

225. Who gave a great feast when his child was weaned?

226. Name the woman who wandered in the desert of Beersheba.

227. Which archer lived in the desert of Paran?

228. Who was the commander of Abimelech's army?

229. What did Abraham complain to Abimelech about?

230. Who did Abraham give sheep and cattle to and make a treaty with?

231. What did Abraham give to Abimelech as a witness that Abraham had dug the well?

232. Name the place where Abraham and Abimelech made a treaty.

233. Which tree did Abraham plant in Beersheba?

234. What did God tell Abraham to do to Isaac?

235. Name the place where Abraham took Isaac for the sacrifice.

236. How many servants did Abraham take with him to sacrifice Isaac?

237. How many days did it take Abraham to reach the land of Moriah?

238. What did Abraham sacrifice on the altar prepared for Isaac in the land of Moriah?

239. What did Abraham name the place where Isaac had to be sacrificed?

240. Who was the first born son of Nahor?

241. At what age did Sarah die?

242. Where did Sarah die?

243. Who is the first person in the Bible who purchased a burial place?

244. From whom did Abraham purchase the burial place for Sarah?

245. For how many pieces of silver shekels did Abraham purchase the burial place from Ephron?

246. What is the name of the burial place that Abraham purchased?

247. Who prayed for a wife for his master's son?

248. Who was the father of Rebecca?

249. Who was a very beautiful young virgin girl mentioned in the book of Genesis?

250. What was the weight of the gold nose ring that Abraham's servant gave Rebecca?

Pentateuch – Genesis

251. What was the weight of the two gold bracelets that Abraham's servant gave Rebecca?

252. Who was the father of Bethuel?

253. Who was the mother of Bethuel?

254. Who was the brother of Rebecca?

255. Who went out to the fields in the evening to meditate?

256. Name the place where Isaac greeted Rebecca.

257. Who was the second wife of Abraham?

258. What was the age of Abraham when he died?

259. Who was the first born son of Ishmael?

260. How old was Ishmael when he died?

261. Who lived in hostility with the other descendants of Abraham?

262. How old was Isaac when he married Rebecca?

263. Who prayed to the Lord for his wife because she was barren?

264. Whose body was red when he was born?

265. Whose body was like a hairy garment when he was born?

266. Who was born with his hand grasping his elder brother's heel?

267. What was the age of Isaac when Esau and Jacob were born?

268. Name the man who was a skilled hunter and who loved outdoor life.

269. Name the man who loved a quiet life and who stayed at home.

270. What name did Esau get after drinking the red stew?

271. Who sold his rights as the first born son?

272. Name the Bible character who despised his birthright.

273. Where did the Lord appear to Isaac?

274. With whom did God reconfirm the promises that He had previously made with Abraham?

275. Who reaped a hundredfold of what he had sowed at Gerar?

276. Who continued to prosper at Gerar and became a very rich man?

277. Who filled up the wells with earth, which Abraham's servants had dug?

278. What are the names of the disputed wells in the valley of Gerar?

279. What is the name of the undisputed well in the valley of Gerar?

280. Who was the adviser of King Abimelech of Gerar?

281. From which name did the city of Beersheba get its name?

282. What was the age of Esau when he got married?

283. What were the names of Esau's wives?

284. Which family's daughter-in-law became their source of grief?

285. What was done in order to fool Isaac into thinking that Jacob was Esau?

286. Name the person who cheated his elder brother two times.

287. Who cried and asked for his father's blessings?

288. Who got the blessing from his father, "You will live by the sword"?

289. What did Esau plan to do to Jacob?

290. Who was the daughter of Ishmael whom Esau married?

291. Who dreamed of a stairway reaching from earth to heaven?

292. Who said, "Surely the Lord is in this place, and I was not aware of it"?

293. At which place did Jacob say, "This is the gate of heaven"?

294. Who had poured oil and dedicated the stone as a pillar to God, which he had placed under his head?

295. What was the city of Bethel called at first?

296. Who named the city of Luz as Bethel?

297. Name the place where Jacob took a vow.

298. Who took a vow, "I will give the Lord a tenth of all that the Lord's gives me"?

299. Who wept aloud after kissing his uncle's daughter?

300. For how many months did Jacob stay with Laban without serving him?

301. What are the names of Laban's daughters?

302. Name the daughter of Laban who had weak eyes.

303. Name the daughter of Laban who had a lovely figure and was very beautiful.

304. Who did Jacob want for a wife in exchange for working seven years?

305. Name the servant girl whom Laban gave to his daughter Leah.

306. What was the name of the servant girl of Rachel?

307. For how many years did Jacob serve Laban for Leah and Rachel?

308. Who was the first born son of Jacob?

309. Who was Jacob's third son?

310. Who said, "I have had a great struggle with my sister, and I have won"?

311. Who said, "How happy I am! The woman will call me happy"?

312. Who hired her husband for her son's mandrakes?

313. What was the name of Leah's daughter?

314. What was the name of Rachel's first son?

315. Who said, "When may I do something for my own household?"

316. What did Jacob ask Laban as compensation for him to stay longer?

317. Which was the tree whose branches Jacob placed in the watering troughs of the flocks?

318. Who cheated Jacob by changing his wages 10 times?

319. Who anointed a pillar at Bethel?

320. Name the woman who stole her father's household gods.

321. For how many days did Laban persuade and catch up with Jacob in the hill country of Gilead?

322. Where did Laban meet Jacob, who had run way from Laban's home?

323. In the Bible, where were tambourines and harps mentioned first?

324. Name the person in the Bible who has mentioned she was having her monthly period.

325. For how many years did Jacob serve Laban for the flocks?

326. Who said, "I suffered from the heat during the day and from the cold at night"?

327. For how many years did Jacob serve Laban?

328. Name the first character in the Bible who grazed his father-in-law's flock.

329. What was the name given by Laban to the stone pillar which was set as a covenant memorial between Jacob and Laban?

330. What was the name given by Jacob to the stone pillar which was set as a covenant memorial between Jacob and Laban?

331. Which covenant memorial is known by three names?

332. By what other name was Galeed known as?

333. Who kissed and blessed his grandchildren and daughters in the early morning?

334. Who said, "This is the camp of God!"?

335. What name did Jacob give to the place where he met the angels of God after departing from Laban?

336. Where did Esau live?

337. With how many men did Esau come to meet Jacob?

338. Name the person who crossed the Jordan River with just one staff.

339. How many female goats were selected by Jacob as a gift for his brother Esau?

340. How many goats and rams were selected by Jacob as a gift for his brother Esau?

341. How many camels were selected by Jacob as a gift for his brother Esau?

342. How many cows and bulls were selected by Jacob as a gift for his brother Esau?

343. How many male and female donkeys were selected by Jacob as a gift for his brother Esau?

344. Name the person who wanted to win his brother with gifts and was looking for his forgiveness.

345. Name the river which Jacob crossed with his wives and children on his way back home.

346. Name the person who struggled with God and men and won.

347. What name was given by the Lord to Jacob at Peniel?

348. Who said, "I have seen God face to face, and I am still alive!?"

349. Name the place where Jacob wrestled with the Lord.

350. What happened to Jacob physically in his wrestling with the angel?

351. Who bowed down seven times to the ground as he approached his brother?

352. Who were the two brothers who met after 20 years and embraced each other and started crying?

353. Who saw his brother's face as if he was seeing the face of God?

354. On being insisted, who had accepted gifts from his brother?

355. Where did Jacob build a place for himself and shelters for his livestock?

356. Who is the father of Shechem?

357. For how many pieces of silver did Jacob buy a plot of ground from the sons of Hamor, where he had pitched his tent?

358. What is the name of the altar that Jacob set at Shechem?

359. Who is the mother of Dinah?

360. Name the person who raped Dinah.

361. Name the person who loved Dinah and spoke tenderly to her.

362. After hearing about Dinah's rape, who spoke nothing and waited for his sons to come back home?

363. Name the person who was the most honored of his entire father's family and was the ruler of city of Shechem.

364. On what condition did the sons of Jacob say they would agree to Shechem's request to marry Dinah?

365. Name the sons of Jacob who attacked the unsuspecting city of Shechem and killed all the males of the city.

366. Who looted the city of Shechem?

367. Where did God tell Jacob to return?

368. What did Jacob ask his household to do?

369. Where did Jacob bury all the foreign gods and the rings?

370. What was the name given to the place in Luz where Jacob built an altar?

371. Who was the nurse of Rebecca?

372. Where was Rebecca's nurse Deborah buried?

373. What name was given to the place where Deborah was buried?

374. Who poured a drink offering and oil on the pillar where God appeared to him?

375. Name the father who changed the name of his son which was given by his mother.

376. What was the name given to Benjamin by his mother?

377. Where did Rachel die?

378. What is the other name of Bethlehem?

379. Name the man who marked a pillar on his wife's tomb.

380. Name the person who slept with his father's concubine.

381. Name the concubine of Jacob whom Reuben slept with?

382. What is the other name of Hebron?

383. At what age did Isaac die?

384. What are the names of the 12 sons of Jacob?

385. Who were the sons of Leah?

386. Who were the sons of Rachel?

387. Who were the sons of Bilhah?

388. Who were the sons of Zilpah?

389. What is the other name of Esau?

390. Who was the daughter of Ishmael whom Esau married?

391. Name the two brothers whose possessions were too great for them to remain together.

392.   Who settled in the hill country of Seir?

393.   Who is the father of the Edomites?

394.   Who discovered the hot springs in the desert while he was grazing the donkeys of his father?

395.   Who was the father of Anah?

396.   Who was the daughter of Anah?

397.   Who was the first king of Edom?

398.   What was the name of Bela's city?

399.   Name the person who defeated Midian in the country of Moab.

400.   What was the name of Hadad's city?

401.   What was the name of Hadar's city?

402.   What was the name of Hadar's wife?

403.   How old was Joseph when his brothers sold him?

404.   Who was loved more than any of his brothers because he had been born to his father in his old age?

405.   For whom did Jacob make an ornate robe?

406.   Name the person who was loved by his father but hated by his brothers.

407.   Name the person for whom it is said, "His brothers were jealous of him, but his father kept the matter in mind."

408.   Name the place where Joseph found his brothers grazing their father's flock.

409.   Who tried to rescue Joseph from his brothers' hands?

410.   Name the person who took the initiative to sell Joseph to the Ishmaelites.

411. For how many silver shekels did Joseph's brothers sell him to the Ishmaelites?

412. Who tore his clothes when he didn't find his brother in the cistern?

413. Name the person who tore his clothes, put on sackcloth and mourned for his son for many days.

414. "All his sons and daughters came to comfort him, but he refused to be comforted." Name the person.

415. To whom did the Midianite sell Joseph?

416. Who was Potiphar?

417. Who was the Adullamite friend of Judah?

418. Who was the first born son of Judah?

419. Who were the 2nd and 3rd sons of Judah?

420. Name the place where Shelah was born?

421. Who was the wife of Er?

422. Name the person who was wicked in the Lord's sight; so the Lord put him to death.

423. Who is mentioned as the first widow in the Bible?

424. Where did Tamar sit dressed up like a prostitute?

425. Who took a pledge until she received her wages?

426. What did Judah leave with Tamar as a pledge?

427. Who were the two sons of Tamar?

428. Name the son of Tamar who had a scarlet thread on his wrist.

429. Name the person who was well built and handsome.

430. Name the woman who took notice of Joseph.

431. What did Joseph leave in Potiphar's wife's hand and run away?

432. What was Joseph falsely accused of?

433. What responsibility did the keeper of the prison give Joseph?

434. Who were the two officials of Pharaoh who had dreams and were sad?

435. What did the three branches and three baskets of bread represent in the dream of the chief cupbearer and the chief baker?

436. Which person, after having his dream interpreted, was restored to his position?

437. After the release of the chief cupbearer, how many years had passed when the Pharaoh had his dream?

438. How many cows did Pharaoh see in his dreams?

439. Name the person whose mind was troubled in the morning.

440. Name the first person in the Bible who had his head shaved.

441. What was the interpretation of Pharaoh's dream?

442. To what position was Joseph promoted?

443. Name the person whom Pharaoh dressed in robes of fine linen.

444. Name the Hebrew man in whose hand Pharaoh put his signet ring.

445. What name did Pharaoh give Joseph?

446. What was Joseph's wife's name?

447. Whose daughter was Asenath?

448. What was the age of Joseph when he entered the service of Pharaoh?

449. How many years had passed since Joseph had the dream and when he entered the service of the Pharaoh?

450. Name the person who stored as much grain as the sand of the sea.

451. Who was the first son of Joseph?

452. Who was the second son of Joseph?

453. How many of Joseph's brother travelled to Egypt to buy grain at the first time?

454. Which son of Jacob didn't go to Egypt to buy grain at the first time?

455. Name the man who recognized his brothers but pretended to be a stranger and spoke harshly to them.

456. What did Joseph tell his brothers to do in order to prove that they were not spies?

457. For how many days did Joseph put his 10 brothers in custody?

458. Who was using an interpreter to talk to his brothers?

459. Name the person whom Joseph bounded in front of his brothers.

460. Who were frightened by seeing their pouch of silver?

461. Who said, "Everything is against me!?"

462. What did Jacob's sons give Joseph as a gift?

463. Who went into his private room and wept there after seeing his younger brother?

464. Name the person who received five times more portion than any of his brothers.

465. What did the steward say would happen to the person with whom the cup was found?

466. In whose sack was the silver cup of Joseph found?

467. Who tore their clothes after the silver cup was found?

468. "The boy cannot leave his father; if he leaves him, his father will die." Name the father and the son.

469. Who guaranteed Benjamin's safety to his father?

470. Who were terrified at their brother's presence?

471. For what purpose did Joseph say he was sent into Egypt?

472. How many years of famine were still to come after Joseph revealed himself to his brothers?

473. How many years of famine had passed when Joseph revealed himself to his brothers?

474. Joseph gave new clothing to all his brothers. What did he give Benjamin?

475. Who was stunned after hearing the news about his son?

476. What convinced Jacob that Joseph was alive?

477. Where did Jacob offer sacrifices to the God of his father Isaac when he left for Egypt?

478. Name the sons of Judah who had died in the land of Canaan.

479. How many of Benjamin's sons had gone to Egypt?

480. How many members of Jacob's family went to Egypt?

481. Where did Joseph meet his father Jacob who had come to Egypt?

482. In what portion of Egypt did Jacob and his descendants settle?

483. How many of his brothers did Joseph present before the Pharaoh?

484. What was the occupation of Jacob and his sons?

485. Name the person who blessed Pharaoh.

486. What was the age of Jacob when he was presented before the Pharaoh?

487. Which district in the land of Goshen did the Pharoah give to Jacob and his sons?

488. Whose land in Egypt hadn't been bought by Joseph?

489. Who did not sell their land to Joseph because they received a regular allotment from Pharaoh and had enough food from the allotment?

490. For how many years did Jacob live in the land of Egypt?

491. At what age did Jacob die?

492. Whom did Jacob bless with his left hand?

493. Who put Ephraim ahead of Manasseh?

494. Name the person to whom Jacob gave one more ridge of land which he took from the Amorites.

495. Who is as turbulent as the waters?

496. Name the person who went up onto his father's bed and defiled it?

497. Who are the two brothers whose swords are the weapons of violence?

498. Who are the two brothers who killed men in their anger?

499. Name the person whom Jacob blessed, "Your brothers will praise you!".

500. Name the person whom Jacob called "a lion's cub."

501.   Who will hold the royal scepter?

502.   Who will wash his garments in wine and his robes in the blood of grapes?

503.   Whose eyes will be darker than wine and teeth whiter than milk?

504.   Who has been blessed by Jacob as, "He will live by the seashore!"?

505.   Who is a rawboned donkey lying down among the sheep pens?

506.   Who is a snake by the roadside and a viper along the path?

507.   Who is the snake that bites the horse's heels?

508.   Who will be attacked by a band of raiders, but he will attack them at their heels?

509.   Whose food will be rich and will provide delicacies fit for a king?

510.   Who is a doe set free that bears beautiful fawns?

511.   Who is a fruitful vine near a spring?

512.   Name the person for whom Jacob said, "With bitterness archers attacked him!".

513.   Whose bow remained steady and arms stayed limber because of the hand of the mighty one of Jacob?

514.   Name the person whom Jacob mentioned as a ravenous wolf.

515.   Who devours the prey in the morning and divides the plunder in the evening?

516.   Name the women who had been buried in the cave of Machpelah.

517. Who threw himself on his father's dead body and wept over him and kissed him?

518. How many days did the physicians take to embalm the body of Jacob?

519. For how many days did the Egyptians mourn for Jacob?

520. Name the place near the Jordan River where the descendants of Jacob lamented for him.

521. For how many days did the descendants of Jacob lament for him at Atad?

522. Name the place where the Canaanites said, "This is a grievous mourning to the Egyptians!".

523. What is the other name of Atad?

524. At what age did Joseph die?

525. Name the son of Manasseh.

526. What did Joseph request the children of Israel?

527. Whose body was placed in a coffin after it had been embalmed?

Who said to whom?

528. "Why are you angry? Why is your face downcast?"

529. "If you do what is right, will you not be accepted?"

530. "Am I my brother's keeper?"

531. "You will be a restless wanderer on earth."

532. "My punishment is more than I can bear."

533. "Today you are driving me from the land, and I will be hidden from your presence; I will be a restless wanderer on earth."

534.   "I have found you righteous in this generation."

535.   "I will bless those who bless you."

536.   "Now then, here is your wife. Take her and go."

537.   "For we are brothers."

538.   "If you go to the left, I will go to the right."

539.   "Give me the people and keep the goods for yourself."

540.   "You will go to your ancestors in peace and be buried at a good old age."

541.   "You are responsible for the wrong I am suffering."

542.   "Your slave is in your hands, do with her whatever you think best."

543.   "Where have you come from and where are you going?"

544.   "Go back to your mistress and submit to her."

545.   "I have now seen the One who sees me."

546.   "If I have found favor in your eyes, my lord, do not pass your servant by."

547.   "Let me get you something to eat, so you can be refreshed and then go on your way."

548.   "Is anything too hard for the Lord?"

549.   "I have two daughters who have never slept with a man."

550.   "We'll treat you worse than them."

551.   "Do you have anyone else here?"

552.   "Hurry and get out of this place, because the Lord is about to destroy the city!"

553.   "Flee for your lives! Don't look back."

554.   "Flee to the mountains or you will be swept away!"

555.   "You have shown great kindness to me in sparing my life."

556.   "I cannot do anything until you reach there."

557.   "I have done this with a clear conscience and clean hands."

558.   "I have kept you from sinning against me."

559.   "He will pray for you and you will live."

560.   "How have I wronged you that you have brought such great guilt upon me and my kingdom?"

561.   "You have done things to me that should never be done."

562.   "What was your reason for doing this?"

563.   "She is the daughter of my father though not of my mother."

564.   "My land is before you; live wherever you like."

565.   "What is the matter? Do not be afraid."

566.   "God is with you in everything you do."

567.   "I am a foreigner and stranger among you."

568.   "You are a mighty prince among us."

569.   "What is that between you and me?"

570.   "Make sure that you do not take my son back there."

571.   "Please give me a little water from your jar."

572.   "Come, you who are blessed by the Lord, why are you standing out here?"

573.   "I will not eat until I have told you what I have to say."

574.   "This is from the Lord; we can say nothing to you one way or the other."

Pentateuch – Genesis

575. "Do not detain me, now that the Lord has granted success to my journey."

576. "May you increase to thousands upon thousands, may your offspring possess the cities of their enemies."

577. "Why have you come to me, since you were hostile to me and sent me away?"

578. "I am now an old man and don't know the day of my death."

579. "Now my son, listen carefully and do what I tell you."

580. "My son, let the curse fall on me."

581. "Come here, my son, and kiss me."

582. "Haven't you reserved any blessing for me?"

583. "What can I possibly do for you, my son?"

584. "Do you have only one blessing, my father?"

585. "Why should I lose both of you in one day?"

586. "You are my own flesh and blood."

587. "Tell me, what your wages should be?"

588. "It's better that I give her to you than to some other man."

589. "Why have you deceived me?"

590. "It is not our custom here to give the younger daughter in marriage before the older one."

591. "Give me children, or I'll die."

592. "Am I in the place of God, who has kept you from having children?"

593. "Send me on my way so I can go back to my own homeland."

594. "You know how much work I've done for you."

595. "If I have found favor in your eyes, please stay. I have learned by divination that the Lord has blessed me because of you."

596. "Name your wages and I will pay them."

597. "The little you had before I came has increased greatly."

598. "The Lord has blessed you wherever I have been."

599. "Don't give me anything."

600. "Go back to the land of your fathers and to your relatives."

601. "Do we still have any share in the inheritance of our father's estate?"

602. "You have done a foolish thing."

603. "I have the power to harm you."

604. "Don't be angry, my lord, that I cannot stand up in your presence."

605. "How have I wronged you that you hunt me down?"

606. "The women are my daughters, the children are my children, and the flocks are my flocks."

607. "May the Lord keep watch between you and me when we are away from each other."

608. "Here is this pillar I have set up between you and me."

609. "Let me go, for it is daybreak."

610. "I will not let you go unless you bless me."

611. "Why do you ask my name?"

612. "I already have plenty, my brother. Keep what you have for yourself."

613. "If I have found favor in your eyes, accept this gift from me."

614. "Please accept the present that was brought to you, for God has been gracious to me and I have all I need."

615. "Let us be on our way; I'll accompany you."

616. "You can settle among us; the land is open to you. Live in it, trade in it, and acquire property in it."

617. "Make the price for the bride and the gift I am to bring as great as you like, and I'll pay whatever you ask me."

618. "These men are friendly towards us."

619. "We are few in number."

620. "Come, I am going to send you to them."

621. "He is our brother, our own flesh and blood."

622. "Come now, let me sleep with you."

623. "What will you give me to sleep with you?"

624. "Let her keep what she has, or we will become a laughingstock."

625. "No one is greater in this house than I am."

626. "How could I do such a wicked thing and sin against God?"

627. "We both had dreams, but there is no one to interpret them."

628. "Do not interpretations belong to God? Tell me your dreams."

629. "Today I am reminded of my shortcoming."

630. "Can we find anyone like this man, one in whom is the spirit of God?"

631. "Only with respect to the throne will I be greater than you."

632. "Why do you just keep looking at each other?"

633. "You are spies! You have come to see where our land is unprotected."

634. "We are all the sons of one man. Your servants are honest men."

635. "You have deprived me of my children."

636. "You will bring my gray head down to the grave in sorrow."

637. "If we had not delayed, we could have gone and returned twice."

638. "As for me, if I am bereaved, I am bereaved."

639. "God be gracious to you, my son."

640. "Why have you repaid good with evil?"

641. "Far be it from your servants to do anything like that!"

642. "God has uncovered your servants' guilt. We are now my lord's slaves."

643. "Do not let me see the misery that would come on my father."

644. "Have everyone leave my presence."

645. "I will give you the best of the land of Egypt and you can enjoy the fat of the land."

646. "Never mind about your belongings."

647. "Don't quarrel on the way!"

648. "Do not be afraid to go down to Egypt, for I will make you into a great nation there."

649. "My years have been few and difficult, and they do not equal the years of the pilgrimage of my fathers."

650. "You have saved our lives. May we find favor in the eyes of our Lord."

651. "His younger brother will be greater than he, and his descendants will become a group of nations."

652. "I am about to die, but God will be with you and take you back to the land of your fathers."

653. "Gather around so I can tell you what will happen to you in days to come."

654. "Please forgive the sins of the servants of the God of your father."

655. "Don't be afraid. Am I in the place of God?"

656. "You intended to harm me, but God intended it for good to accomplish what is now being done, the saving of many lives."

657. "Don't be afraid. I will provide for you and your children."

658. "God will surely come to your aid, and then you must carry my bones up from this place."

Exodus

Exodus

The book of Exodus consists mainly of two genres, Narrative History and Laws. It was written by Moses at around 1450-1410 B.C. The key personalities include Moses, Miriam, Pharaoh, Pharaoh's daughter, Aaron and Joshua. It was written to record the events of Israel's deliverance from slavery in Egypt. It describes the events to the reader in chronological order and also lists the Laws that God gave the Israelites, in order to guide them in their relationship with Him.

- Chapters 1-7 of Exodus introduces Moses and the Israelites in bondage in Egypt. This setting is approximately 400 years after Joseph and his families were living in Goshen at the end of Genesis. God protects baby Moses and spares his life, as Moses is adopted by Pharaoh's daughter and is raised as an Egyptian. God calls Moses with a special revelation, through a burning bush to release His people from slavery in Egypt. Moses obeys and with his brother Aaron, confronts Pharaoh to let God's people go free, but Pharaoh ignores the warning.

- Chapters 7-13, Moses through the power of God releases 10 plagues of different sorts on the land of Egypt which included, turning water to blood, plagues of insects, boils, and hail. Finally, the death of every first-born son, this included the death of Pharaoh's eldest who would have someday inherited the kingdom of Egypt. However, the Israelites obeyed God and followed the ordinance of the Passover and God spared them.

- Chapters 14-18 describe the Exodus or *"Exit"* from Egypt. Pharaoh can no longer endure the plagues that God poured on Egypt and himself and allows them to leave. Moses and the Israelites escape making it to the Red Sea. Shortly after, Pharaoh changes his mind and pursues them. But God destroys his army with the sea.

- Chapters 19-24, Moses presents all of the Laws to all the people at Mt. Sinai as God has commanded.

- Chapters 25-40, Moses gives the Israelites the tabernacle, priest and worship instructions.

Pentateuch – Exodus

1.   How many chapters are there in this book?

2.   How many verses are there in this book?

3.   Who is the author of this book?

4.   When was this book written?

5.   Name the 12 sons of Jacob who went with him to Egypt.

6.   How many people went to Egypt who directly descended from Jacob?

7.   Who were being oppressed with forced labor?

8.   Name the cities built by the Israelites to serve as supply centers for the king.

9.   Who multiplied and spread more on being oppressed?

10.   Name the two mid-wives who helped the Hebrew women.

11.   What did Pharaoh tell the Hebrew midwives to do?

12.   Who were vigorous women?

13.   What did the Lord give the midwives for the fear of the Lord?

14.   Which tribe did Moses belong to?

15.   For how many months did Moses' mother hide him?

16.   Name the girl who hid behind the reed to see what would happen to her brother?

17.   Name the woman who was paid by the princess for feeding her own baby.

18.   Who named Moses?

19.   Name the Hebrew child who was raised as the son of Pharaoh's daughter.

20.   Who did Moses kill when he saw a Hebrew being beaten?

21. Where did Moses run away from the fear of the king?

22. How many daughters did Jethro have?

23. Who was Jethro?

24. Name the daughter of Jethro who married Moses.

25. What was the name of Moses' first son?

26. Who said, "I am a foreigner in this land?"

27. What was the name of Moses' father-in-law?

28. Which mountain is known as the mountain of God?

29. How did God catch Moses' attention?

30. To whom did the angel of the Lord appear from within a bush?

31. Name the man who covered his face, because he was afraid to look at God.

32. Name the prophet who asked the name of the Lord.

33. How was Moses to reply when the children of Israel asked for the name of God?

34. How many days' journey in the desert are the Israelites to take to offer a sacrifice to the Lord?

35. Whom did the Israelite women plunder?

36. What was Moses holding when he talked to God?

37. How many miracles did God ask Moses to perform before the Israelites?

38. Name the man who was a poor speaker, slow and hesitant.

39. Who was the spokesperson for Moses?

40. Which tribe did Aaron belong to?

41. Who would be like a God for Aaron, telling him what to say?

42. Name the thing that God asked Moses to take with him which would perform miracles.

43. Name the first woman who sat on a donkey.

44. Name the person whom the Lord tried to kill when he was at a camping place on the way to Egypt.

45. Name the woman who cut off the foreskin of her son with a sharp stone.

46. Who said, "You are a husband of blood to me?"

47. Name the man who met Moses at the holy mountain and kissed him.

48. Name the man who said, "I don't know the Lord."

49. What did Moses and Aaron demand from the king?

50. What did the Israelites use in place of straw to make bricks?

51. Who beat the Israelites for not making the same number of bricks?

52. What did the Pharaoh command the slave drivers when Moses first requested him to let the people of Israel go?

53. Name the person to whom God did not make himself known by his holy name.

54. To whom did God promise to give the land of Canaan?

55. Whose spirit was broken by their cruel slavery?

56. Name the person to whom God said, "I am the Lord."

57. How many sons did Reuben have?

58. How many sons did Simeon have?

59. How many sons did Levi have?

60. For how many years did Levi live?

61. Who married his father's sister Jochebed?

62. What were the names of Moses and Aaron's parents?

63. For how many years did Amram live?

64. What was the name of Aaron's wife?

65. What was the name of Aaron's sons?

66. What was the name of Aminadab's daughter and Nahshon's sister?

67. Who was Phinehas' father?

68. Who was like God to the Pharaoh?

69. Who was going to speak for Moses as a prophet?

70. What was the age of Moses and Aaron when they went to speak to the King?

71. What was the first miracle performed by Aaron?

72. What was Pharaoh's reaction when his magicians imitated the plague of turning water into blood?

73. Who dug along the Nile to get drinking water?

74. Name the river which was turned into blood by Moses and Aaron.

75. Name all the disasters that struck Egypt.

76. Who said, "God has done this"?

77. Name the area where the people of Israel lived in Egypt.

78. Who said, "I will make a distinction between my people and your people"?

79. What did God ask Moses and Aaron to throw in the air in order to produce boils?

80. Name the disaster due to which the Egyptian magicians were not able to appear before Moses.

81. Name the crops that were destroyed due to boils.

82. Name the crops that were not destroyed by boils.

83. Name the two men who were driven out of the king's presence.

84. Which wind picked up the locusts and blew them away?

85. Where did the west wind blow away the locusts?

86. For how many days did darkness cover the land of Egypt?

87. What would Moses never see again according to Pharaoh?

88. What did God ask the people of Israel to go and ask from their neighbours?

89. Who was considered as a very great man by the Egyptian officials and the people of Egypt?

90. Where does the Bible first mention a dog?

91. Name the festival celebrated by Israelites in the first month of each year.

92. On which day do the Israelites have to choose a lamb or a goat for their household?

93. On which day do the Israelites have to kill those lambs or the goats they have chosen?

94. What is to be eaten along with the roasted meat during the Passover festival?

95. What did the Lord ask the people of Israel to eat quickly?

96. For how many days did the Lord ask the Israelites to eat bread made without yeast?

97. What did Moses ask the Israelites to dip in the bowl containing the animal's blood, and wipe the blood on the doorposts and the beam above the door?

98. Who carried on their shoulders their baking pans with unleavened dough, wrapped in clothing?

99. Where did the Israelites set out on foot from Rameses?

100. How many men left from Egypt?

101. For how many years did the Israelites live in the land of Egypt?

102. What must not be eaten by any foreigner, but can be eaten by any slave that the Israelites have bought if circumcised?

103. Which meat was not allowed to be eaten outside the house?

104. For how many days is the Passover meal to be eaten?

105. Name the first month of the Hebrew calendar.

106. Which was the shortest way to Canaan?

107. Why didn't God lead the Israelites by the way of the land of the Philistines?

108. Whose body did the Israelites take with them when they left Egypt?

109. Name the place where Israelites first camped when they left Egypt.

110. How did God lead the Israelites during the day and during the night?

111. Where did God ask the Israelites to camp between Migdol and the Red sea near Baal Zephon?

112. How many finest chariots were arranged by the king of Egypt to pursue the Israelites?

113. What stood in between the army of Israel and the army of Egypt?

114. By what means did God cause the Red Sea to go back?

115. For whom did the waters stand as wall?

116. Who stood panicked in between the sea?

117. In the song of Moses, whose mighty men are trembling?

118. Name the sister of Aaron who was a prophet.

119. Name the first prophetess who danced in the Bible.

120. Name the first female singer of the Bible.

121. After crossing the Red Sea where did Moses lead the people of Israel?

122. Where did the Israelites find the bitter water?

123. After crossing the Red Sea, name the place where the Israelites first complained to Moses.

124. What problem did the Israelites encounter at Marah?

125. What did Moses throw into the water so as to make it fit for drinking?

126. Where did the Israelites find the 12 springs and 70 palm trees?

127. Which desert is found between Elim and Sinai?

128. Name the bird that God provided for the Israelites when they complained for meat?

129. What did God provide for the Israelites when they complained for bread?

130. How many kilos of manna was gathered by each person?

131. Who named the food provided by God as manna?

132. How many kilos of manna were kept in the jar to preserve for the descendents of Israel to see?

133. How many years did the children of Israel eat manna?

134. Where did Israelites camp after moving from the Sin Desert?

135. What did Moses name the place where the Israelites complained and put the Lord to test when they asked, "Is the Lord with us or not?"

136. How did God solve the thirst problem of the Israelites?

137. Where did the Amalekites come and attack the Israelites?

138. Who stood beside Moses to hold up his arms, until evening?

139. What did Moses name the altar he built?

140. God asked Moses to write an account on victory against which army?

141. What was the name of Moses' second son?

142. Who gave Moses advice to appoint some leaders for the people of Israel who can settle their disputes?

143. When did the people of Israel reach the Sinai desert after leaving Egypt?

144. Where did the people of Israel camp at Sinai desert?

145.   What did God want Israel to be?

146.   Which mountain was covered with smoke because the Lord had come down on it with fire?

147.   For how many generations will God punish those who hate him?

148.   For how many generations will God show his love to those who love him and obey his commands?

149.   How many of the Ten Commandments deal with our relationship to other humans?

150.   What physical phenomena accompanied the giving of the Ten Commandments?

151.   What kind of altar did God ask to build for him?

152.   For how many years can a Hebrew slave serve an Israelite?

153.   When can an Israelite pierce his slave's ear?

154.   What was the punishment for one who hits his father or his mother?

155.   What was the punishment of cursing one's father mother?

156.   What was the punishment for the one who hurts a pregnant woman and loses her child?

157.   What was the punishment of kidnapping?

158.   What was the punishment for a bull if it gores someone to death?

159.   What happened to the owner of an animal that killed a person if the owner knew that the animal previously had a record of violence?

160.   What was the punishment if a bull killed a male or female slave?

161. What was the punishment for having a sexual relation with an animal?

162. By what time a pledged cloak of a neighbour was to be returned?

163. What blinds those who see and twists the words of the innocent?

164. What was the Sabbath for?

165. How many times in a year did the Israelites have to celebrate a festival for the Lord?

166. The fat of the festival offerings must not be kept until what time?

167. What kind of milk should a young goat not be cooked in?

168. What kind of women did the Lord say will not be in Israel if the Israelites worshiped the Lord?

169. Who set up an altar at the foot of the mountain with twelve stone pillars representing the twelve tribes of Israel?

170. Who ate and drank when they saw God?

171. On which day did the Lord call Moses from within the cloud?

172. For how many days did Moses stay on Mountain Sinai?

173. Name the person who stayed with the Lord on the Mountain for 40 days and for 40 nights.

174. Which wood was used to make the Covenant box?

175. What was the dimension of the Covenant box?

176. How many gold rings were there in the Covenant box?

177. What was the dimension of the atonement cover?

178.   What was the dimension of the table?

179.   What is to be placed at all times on the table of the Covenant box?

180.   Which metal was used to make the lamp stand for the sacred tent?

181.   How much pure gold was used to make the lamp stand and all its accessories?

182.   How many curtains were there in the Tabernacle?

183.   What were the curtains of Tabernacle made of?

184.   Which hair was used to make the cover for the Tabernacle?

185.   What was the dimension of each frame in the Tabernacle?

186.   How many projections were there for each frame of the Tabernacle?

187.   How many frames were there in total in the Tabernacle?

188.   How many crossbars were there in the Tabernacle?

189.   What divided the Holy place from the Most Holy place?

190.   What was built in the Tabernacle with the same length and width?

191.   What was the dimension of the altar in the Tabernacle?

192.   Who were selected for the priesthood?

193.   Which prophet made garments for his brother to give him dignity and honor?

194.   What are the garments of the High Priest?

195.   What was engraved on the stones for the breastplate?

196. Which two objects were kept in the breastplate of the High Priest?

197. What were put around the hem of the robe of the High Priest?

198. What was engraved on the gold plate of the High Priest?

199. Who must burn fragrant incense on the altar every morning?

200. While taking census, how much shekel was to be given by all those who were 20 years old or more as an offering to the Lord?

201. How much gerahs is one shekel?

202. What would happen to a priest if he made an offering without washing?

203. Who did the Lord call and appoint to make the items for the tabernacle and the priesthood?

204. Name the artistic designer who was filled with the spirit of God, wisdom, understanding, knowledge and all kinds of skill?

205. Who was the father of Bezalel?

206. Which tribe did Bezalel belong to?

207. Which tribe did Oholiab belong to?

208. Who was the father of Oholiab?

209. What did the people request of Aaron while Moses was on Mount Sinai?

210. Who rallied to Moses when he said, "Whoever is for the Lord, come to me"?

211. Which tribe killed 3000 people of Israel because of the Golden Calf?

212. How many people were killed because of the Golden Calf?

213. How did the Lord speak to Moses?

214. Who said to the Lord, "Blot me out of the book you have written"?

215. Where did the Israelites strip off their ornaments?

216. Name the tent that Moses used to pitch outside the camp.

217. Who was the helper of Moses?

218. Who was the father of Joshua?

219. Who said, "If your presence does not go with us, do not send us up from here"?

220. Who said, "Now show me your glory"?

221. Who cut the second set of tablets of stone?

222. Who wrote the commandments on the second tablets?

223. Name the first man whose face shined.

224. Name the person whose face was radiant.

225. Name the person who put a veil over his face.

226. Name the temple which was carried by men.

227. On which day are the Israelites not allowed to light a fire in their dwellings?

228. How much gold was used to build the Tabernacle?

229. How much silver was obtained from those communities who were counted in the census?

230. How much bronze was obtained from wave offering?

231. What did the onyx stones on the shoulder pieces of the ephod represent?

232. Which garment of the High Priest was square in size?

233. What happened when Moses finished erecting the Tabernacle?

234. How did the Israelites know when to move?

Who said to whom?

235. "Why have you returned so early today?"

236. "Where is he? Why did you leave him?"

237. "Invite him to have something to eat."

238. "The place where you are standing is holy ground."

239. "I AM WHO I AM."

240. "What is that in your hand?"

241. "Who gave human beings their mouth?"

242. "I will help you speak and will teach you what to say."

243. "Please send someone else."

244. "He will be glad to see you."

245. "It will be as if he were your mouth and as if you were God to him."

246. "Why are you taking the people away from their labor? Get back to your work!"

247. "Lazy, that's what you are – lazy!"

248. "May the Lord look on you and judge you! You have put a sword in their hand to kill us."

249. "Lord, why have you brought trouble on this people? Is this why you sent me?"

250. "I speak with faltering lips."

251. "It will be as you say, so that you may know there is no one like the Lord our God."

252. "This time I have sinned, the Lord is in the right, and I and my people are in the wrong."

253. "I will let you go; you don't have to stay any longer."

254. "How long will this man be a snare to us?"

255. "Do you not yet realize that Egypt is ruined?"

256. "Clearly you are bent on evil."

257. "I have sinned against the Lord your God and against you."

258. "Now forgive my sin once more and pray to the Lord your God to take this deadly plague away from me."

259. "Make sure you do not appear before me again! The day you see my face you will die."

260. "Just as you say, I will never appear before your eyes."

261. "Was it because there were no graves in Egypt that you brought us to the desert to die?"

262. "Do not be afraid. Stand firm and you will see the deliverance the Lord will bring you today."

263. "The Lord will fight for you; you need only to be still."

264. "Why are you crying out to me?"

265. "What you are doing is not good. You and these people who come to you will only wear yourselves out."

266. "The work is too heavy for you; you cannot handle it alone."

267. "Listen now to me and I will give you some advice."

268. "Let them bring every difficult case to you; the simple cases they can decide themselves."

269. "Do not have God speak to us or we will die."

270. "You have committed a great sin."

271. "If you are pleased with me, teach me your ways so I may know you and continue to find favor with you."

272. "You cannot see my face."

273. "I know you by name and you have found favor with me."

274. "The Lord, the Lord, the compassionate and gracious God, slow to anger, abounding in love and faithfulness."

275. "If I have found favor in your eyes, then let the Lord go with us."

276. "Obey what I command you today."

277. "Be careful not to make a treaty with those who live in the land where you are going."

Leviticus

Leviticus

Leviticus is composed of two basic genres, Narrative History and Law. It was written by Moses about 1445-1444 B.C. The setting of Leviticus mainly appears to have taken place at Mt. Sinai. The key personalities of Leviticus include Moses, Aaron, Nadab, Abihu, Eleazar and Ithamar.

It was written to draw the Israelites to the understanding of the infinite holiness of God, and that He desires them to act in a holy manner towards Himself. In doing this, God gives them many instructions to carry out. It describes Moses giving procedural instructions for the Israelites, especially to the Levitical priests, about how they are to carry out offerings, ceremonies and celebrations. The word *"Holy"* is mentioned more times in Leviticus, than any other book in the Bible.

- Chapters 1-7, Sacrifice and Offerings are laid out for priests and individuals in detail. These passages also describe how to use the altar for the sacrifices and offerings to God.

- Chapters 8-10, Moses describes the instructions for the Levitical Priesthood, since Israel is to be *"a kingdom of priests"* (Ex. 19:6). He does this from the doorway to his tent. Moses consecrates his brother Aaron and his sons who are priests.

- Chapters 11-15 Moses teaches the importance and procedures for things that are unclean. These include food, diseases, animals, insects, dead bodies, birth, cleaning and many others. God's purpose of all this is to protect His people from illnesses and diseases that come from these sources.

- Chapter 16, Moses gives instruction about the Day of Atonement. This was the day out of the year that the High Priest cleanses and prepares himself ceremonially to meet with God. This ceremony only takes place once a year. The High Priest enters into the Holy of Holiest and offers a sacrifice to God for sins on behalf of the entire nation of Israel.

- Chapters 17-27 pertain to the laws that apply generally for living a holy life. These are the many laws including sexual immorality, idolatry, land laws, more priestly laws, religious festivals and celebrations, the Sabbath year and the year of Jubilee.

Pentateuch – Leviticus

1. How many chapters are there in this book?

2. How many verses are there in this book?

3. Who is the author of this book?

4. When was this book written?

5. How many types of offerings are mentioned in the book of Leviticus?

6. What are the 5 types of offerings mentioned in the book of Leviticus?

7. What are the three primary peace offerings?

8. What living things could be offered as a burnt offering?

9. Who sprinkled blood on the altar?

10. Which type of flour is to be used as a grain offering to the Lord?

11. In which type of offering was incense used?

12. What things are required for grain offerings?

13. Which priests do the remainder of the grain offerings belong to?

14. What should every grain offering that is to be offered to the Lord not be made of?

15. What was not to be included in any grain offering?

16. In which type of offering was salt used?

17. How should the sacrificial animal be?

18. What should a person bring to the Lord if he could not afford a Lamb?

19. In which type of offering can a female flock without any defect be offered?

20. What was a priest to bring as a sin offering if he sins unintentionally?

21. In order to make restitution what did a person who sinned unintentionally add to the offering?

22. What must be kept burning?

23. What was done to the clay pot in which the meat for sin offering was cooked?

24. What offering was made as an expression of thankfulness?

25. In which offering are loaves of bread made with the offering?

26. For how many days could the thanksgiving offering sacrifice be eaten which may be the result of a vow or a freewill offering?

27. Who cannot eat a fellowship offering belonging to the Lord?

28. Who was given a share of the offerings?

29. How many days did the consecration ceremonies for Aaron and his sons last?

30. Which two sons of Aaron offered strange fire before the Lord?

31. Which sons of a priest died in the presence of the Lord?

32. Who took the body of Aaron's sons outside the camp, away from the front of the sanctuary?

33. Who was the father of Mishael and Elzaphan?

34. Name the uncle of Aaron.

35. What were Aaron and his sons not allowed to drink?

36. What kind of animals did the Lord command the Israelites to eat?

37. Name the animals that only chew cud but do not have a divided hoof.

38. Name the animal that has a divided hoof but does not chew cud.

39. What was necessary in the type of creatures in the sea which the Israelites were allowed to eat?

40. For how many days will a woman who gives birth to a son be ceremonially unclean, just as she is unclean during her monthly period?

41. For how many days would a woman who gave birth to a son wait to be purified from bleeding?

42. On what day was a baby boy to be circumcised?

43. For how many days would a woman who gave birth to a daughter be ceremonially unclean, just as she is unclean during her monthly period?

44. How many days would a woman who gave birth to a daughter wait to be purified from bleeding?

45. Who should examine a man or woman who has white spots on the skin?

46. What type of clothes should a person wear who had an infectious disease?

47. Who should shave off all his hair from head, beard, eyebrows and rest of his body?

48. Who was involved in the ceremonial cleansing of the leper?

49. Who should inspect whether there is mildew in a person's house or not?

50.   What was to be done to a house in which leprosy continued to spread?

51.   How many male goats were to be taken from the Israelite community for sin offering?

52.   Israel community offered two male goats for sin offering and had to cast lots for the goats. One lot was for the Lord and who was the other for?

53.   Over which creature did Aaron confess all the iniquities of the Israelites, and send it away into the wilderness?

54.   What was used for the sin offering of Aaron and his household?

55.   How many times did Aaron sprinkle the bull's blood on the atonement cover?

56.   How often was atonement made for the Israelites?

57.   What is the life of every living thing?

58.   What is said of sexual relations with someone of the same sex?

59.   Why are we to be holy?

60.   The Lord commanded the Israelites not to reap to the very edges of the field or gather the gleanings of the harvest or not to pick up the grapes that have fallen in the vineyard. For whom did the Lord ask to leave these things?

61.   What is that phrase which Jesus considered as one of the greatest commandments?

62.   What phrase prohibits body piercing and tattoos?

63.   When did the Israelites begin the Lord's Passover?

64.   Which festival of the Israelites begins on the 15th day of the 1st month?

65.   Which festival of Israelites begins on the 1st day of the 7th month?

66.   When did the Israelites begin their Day of Atonement?

67.   When did the Israelites begin the Festival of Tabernacles?

68.   For how many days do the festival of Tabernacles last?

69.   In the time of Moses, a man was stoned to death, who blasphemed and cursed the name of God. Name the mother of this man.

70.   Who was put in custody until the will of the Lord should be made?

71.   How often did the Year of Jubilee occur?

72.   In how many years could the owner of a house retain the right of redemption if he sold his house in a walled city?

73.   Who could redeem one that was sold?

74.   What is the official standard for setting a male free who is 20 – 60 years old and who has been given to the Lord in fulfillment of a special vow?

75.   What is the official standard for setting a female free who is 20 – 60 years old and who has been given to the Lord in fulfillment of a special vow?

76.   What is the official standard for setting a male free who is 5 – 20 years old and who has been given to the Lord in fulfillment of a special vow?

77.   What is the official standard for setting a female free who is 5 – 20 years old and who has been given to the Lord in fulfillment of a special vow?

Pentateuch – Leviticus

78. What is the official standard for setting a male and female free who is 1 month – 5 years old and who has been given to the Lord in fulfillment of a special vow?

79. What is the official standard for setting a male and female free who is 60 years old or more and who has been given to the Lord in fulfillment of a special vow?

80. How many silver shekels for a homer were to be given if a person dedicates to the Lord part of their family land?

| 70 | Master Bible Quiz – Volume - I

Numbers

Numbers

The book of Numbers is largely Narrative History as far as its genre. It was written by Moses about 1450-1410 B.C. Key personalities include Moses, Aaron, Miriam, Joshua, Caleb Eleazer, Korah and Balaam.

The purpose of the book of Numbers is to tell about how Israel prepared to enter the Promised Land, but sinned and was punished. It describes Moses taking two population censuses, hence the name Numbers.

- Chapters 1-9, the Israelites are preparing for their journey and entry into the Promised land. Moses begins by taking a census of all the tribes, primarily to see how many men are available and in shape for military service. Next, Moses dedicates the Levites and instructs the Nazirite vows and laws. During this time, the Israelites celebrate the 2nd Passover one year after their exit from bondage.

- Chapters 10-12, the Israelites travel from the wilderness in Sinai to approach the Promised land. The people complain about their food, God gives them quail, and because of their greed, He also sends a plague. Miriam and Aaron learn a lesson about whom God places in leadership.

- Chapters 13-19, we see severe punishment for disobedience and unfaithfulness to God. Moses sends out 12 spies to perform reconnaissance on the Promised Land. The 12 spies return and only two of them bring good news. The people fear the occupants and rebel against taking the land. For this God punishes them and sends them into the wilderness for forty years to roam.

• The last chapters of Numbers, from 20-36, the new generation of Israelites again attempt to enter the land to take it as God's promise. This time they easily destroy two nations that confront them as they are entering. Balak uses his prophet Balaam to learn to seduce the Israelites to worship Baal. Because of this disobedience, about 24,000 people die, including Balaam. Before the book of Numbers ends, Moses again conducts a census, and Joshua assumes the leadership of Israel in place of Moses who is banned from the Promised Land, due to his disobedience.

1. How many chapters are there in this book?

2. How many verses are there in this book?

3. Who is the author of this book?

4. When was this book written?

5. What was the least age for men to go to war during the time of Moses?

6. How many men were there in total when the Israelites took the first census after leaving Egypt?

7. At the time of Moses, which ancestral tribe of Israel was not counted along with the others?

8. Who was appointed to be in charge of the Tabernacle of the covenant law - over all its furnishings and everything belonging to it?

9. Who had to set up their tents around the tabernacle?

10. Who was the leader of the people of Judah?

11. Who was the leader of the people of Issachar?

12. Who was the leader of the people of Zebulun?

13. The division of which tribe shall march first?

14. Which tribes camped east of the tabernacle?

15. Who was the leader of the people of Reuben?

16. Who was the leader of the people of Simeon?

17. Who was the leader of the people of Gad?

18. Which tribes camped south of the tabernacle?

19. Who was the leader of the people of Ephraim?

20. Who was the leader of the people of Manasseh?

21.   Who was the leader of the people of Benjamin?

22.   Which tribes camped west of the tabernacle?

23.   Who was the leader of the people of Dan?

24.   Who was the leader of the people of Asher?

25.   Who was the leader of the people of Naphtali?

26.   Which tribes camped north of the tabernacle?

27.   Who was the firstborn son of Aaron?

28.   Name the place where Nadab and Abihu were killed when they offered unholy fire to the Lord.

29.   Which sons of Aaron continued as priests after their brothers died?

30.   Who was the father of Gershon, Kohath and Merari?

31.   What was the total number of all the males, a month old or more who were counted from the Gershomite clans?

32.   Who was the leader of the families of the Gershomites?

33.   What was the total number of all the males, a month old or more who were counted from the Kohathite clans?

34.   Whose duty was it to take care of the ark, table, candlestick, altars and the vessels of the sanctuary?

35.   Who was the leader of the families of the Kohathite clans?

36.   Who was the chief leader of the Levites?

37.   What was the total number of all the males, a month old or more who were counted from the Merarite clans?

38.   Who was the leader of the families of the Merarite clans?

39.   Where did Moses, Aaron and his sons camp?

40. What was the total number of Levites counted by Moses and Aaron according to their clans, including every male a month old or more?

41. What was the total number of firstborn males of the Israelites, a month old or more?

42. How much silver did Moses collect from the firstborn of Israelites according to the sanctuary shekel?

43. Who had the oversight of things in the tabernacle?

44. What was the total number of men from 30 – 50 years of age of the Kohathites who came to serve in the work at the tent of meeting?

45. What was the total number of men from 30 – 50 years of age of the Gershomites who came to serve in the work at the tent of meeting?

46. What was the total number of men from 30 – 50 years of age of the Merarites who came to serve in the work at the tent of meeting?

47. At the time of Moses, how many men came to do the work of serving and carrying the tent of the Lord's presence?

48. If the spirit of jealousy came on a man who suspected his wife committing adultery, what was the wife made to drink?

49. What was the vow of the Nazarite?

50. Who was to say, "The Lord bless you, and keep you. The Lord makes his face shine on you..." when blessing Israel?

51. Name the man and his tribe who brought his offering on the first day of the dedication of the altar.

52. What was the weight of each silver plate that the leaders of each tribe of Israel brought for the dedication of the altar?

53.   What was the weight of each sprinkling bowl that the leaders of each tribe of Israel brought for the dedication of the altar?

54.   How much did the silver dishes altogether weigh which were presented by the leaders of the tribes of Israel on the day of the dedication of the altar?

55.   What was the weight of each gold dish that was filled with incense?

56.   What did Moses hear when he went into the tabernacle after the dedicatory offering?

57.   Which tribe was sprinkled with the water of cleansing and who shaved their whole bodies in order to purify themselves?

58.   Whom did the Lord take in place of all the firstborn sons in Israel?

59.   What age group of Levites performed the services of the Tabernacle?

60.   What did the Israelites celebrate on the 14th day of the first month?

61.   Where did the Israelites celebrate their first Passover festival after leaving Egypt?

62.   What covered the Tabernacle when it was set up?

63.   How many silver trumpets were made by Moses?

64.   Who were to gather before Moses when both the trumpets are sounded?

65.   Who were to gather before Moses when only one trumpet is sounded?

66.   Who were allowed to blow the trumpets?

67.   When the Israelites moved, which tribe went first?

68. One of Moses' brother-in-law's name is mentioned in the Bible. Who is he?

69. What did Moses say whenever the Covenant Box set out?

70. What did Moses say whenever the Covenant Box came to rest?

71. Name the place where the people complained about their hardships in the hearing of the Lord and the fire of the Lord burned and consumed some of the outskirts of the camp.

72. What did manna look like?

73. When was manna provided?

74. Name the person who asked, "Did I conceive all these people? Did I give them birth?"

75. On how many men did God put His spirit to help Moses carry the burden of the people?

76. For how many days did the Israelites eat meat in the wilderness?

77. Name the two elders of Israel who were in the camp and in whom the Spirit of the Lord rested.

78. Name the person who was Moses' helper since he was a young man.

79. What was the least quantity of quails that the Israelites gathered?

80. What did the Lord send while the meat was still between the teeth of Israelites?

81. Name the place where the anger of the Lord burned against the people who had craved for other food while the meat was still between their teeth.

82. What does Kibroth Hattaavah mean?

83.   Who was humble above all men, who were on the face of the earth?

84.   For whom did Lord give witness that, "He is faithful in all my house"?

85.   Name the person to whom Lord speaks clearly but not in riddles.

86.   What judgment fell on Miriam?

87.   For how many days was Miriam sent out of the camp?

88.   Name the place where Miriam was struck with leprosy.

89.   From where did Moses send out spies to explore the land of Canaan?

90.   Who went as a spy from the tribe of Reuben?

91.   Who was the father of Shammau?

92.   Who went as a spy from the tribe of Simeon?

93.   Who was the father of Shaphat?

94.   Who was the father of Caleb?

95.   To which tribe did Caleb belong?

96.   Who went as a spy from the tribe of Issachar?

97.   Who was the father of Igal?

98.   Who was the father of Hosea?

99.   To which tribe did Joshua belong?

100.   Who went as a spy from the tribe of Benjamin?

101.   Who was the father of Palti?

102.   Who went as a spy from the tribe of Zebulun?

103.   Who was the father of Gaddiel?

104. Who went as a spy from the tribe of Manasseh?

105. Who was the father of Gaddi?

106. Who went as a spy from the tribe of Dan?

107. Who was the father of Ammiel?

108. Who went as a spy from the tribe of Asher?

109. Who was the father of Sethur?

110. Who went as a spy from the tribe of Naphtali?

111. Who was the father of Nahbi?

112. Who went as a spy from the tribe of Gad?

113. Who was the father of Geuel?

114. How many men did Moses send to explore the land of Canaan?

115. By what other name was Joshua also known as?

116. Who changed the name of Hosea to Joshua?

117. How far did the spies sent by Moses explore the land of Canaan.

118. Name the sons of Anak who lived in Hebron?

119. How many years before Zoan, in Egypt, was Hebron built?

120. What did the spies bring back to Moses from the land of Canaan?

121. Name the place where the Israelite spies cut off the cluster of grapes.

122. How many days did the spies explore the land of Canaan?

123. Who among the spies silenced the people of Israel in front of Moses?

124. On their way to Canaan where did the Israelites weep aloud for a whole night?

125. Name the place where the Israelites told each other, "We should choose a leader and go back to Egypt."

126. Name the Israelite spies who had torn their clothes.

127. Who said, "If the Lord delights in us, then he will bring us into this land, and give it to us and the Lord is with us; fear them not"?

128. Who disobeyed and tested the Lord ten times?

129. Those over what age would die in the wilderness?

130. How many years would the Israelites wander in the wilderness?

131. What happened to those who searched out the land but brought back the report of unbelief?

132. What happened to the man who gathered sticks on the Sabbath?

133. Who became insolent and rose up against Moses?

134. Who was the father of Dathan and Abiram?

135. To which tribe did Korah belong?

136. How many appointed members of the council joined hands with Korah and Dathan and came as a group to oppose Moses?

137. What happened to Korah and his followers?

138. How many men were consumed by the fire from the Lord when the earth swallowed Korah and his men?

139. How many rods were laid before the Lord in the tabernacle?

140. How many staffs did Moses place before the Lord's Covenant Box?

141. Whose stick sprouted, budded, blossomed and produced ripe almonds?

142. What did the Lord ask Moses to do with Aaron's sprouted stick?

143. Who was not to receive an inheritance in the land of Canaan?

144. What was the share of the Levites among the Israelites?

145. Who gave a tenth of the tithe as a special contribution to the Lord?

146. What were the Levites to give to Aaron the priest?

147. Which animal was used for the cleansing of the priests?

148. Where did Miriam die?

149. Why wasn't Moses allowed to bring the people of Israel into the Promised Land?

150. Name the place where the Lord announced that Moses and Aaron would not lead the people of Israel into the land of Canaan.

151. Where did Aaron die?

152. For how many days did the Israelites mourn for Aaron?

153. Upon whom did Moses put Aaron's garments before Aaron died?

154. Name the place where the Israelites completely destroyed the Canaanites and their cities.

155. What is the meaning of Hormah in Hebrew?

156.   From which metal did Moses make the snake and put it on a pole, so that the people may be healed by the snake bite?

157.   What remedy was given to those bitten by snakes?

158.   Which river flows in the wilderness and extends into Amorite territory?

159.   Which river is the border of Moab, between Moab and Amorites?

160.   Name the place where the leaders of the Israelites dug a well with a royal scepter and by their walking sticks.

161.   Which was the capital city of the Amorite King Sihon?

162.   Name the place where King Og of Bashan marched out with his army to attack the Israelites.

163.   Who was the father of Balak?

164.   Who was the father of Balaam?

165.   Who was the Moabite King who summoned a prophet to put a curse on the Israelites?

166.   When Balaam went with the Moabite leaders, who stood in his path?

167.   How many servants were with Balaam when he went to Moab?

168.   How many times did Balaam beat his donkey?

169.   Who said, "A donkey has made a fool of me"?

170.   Name the place where Balak took Balaam to show him the outskirts of the Israelite camp.

171.   Who said, "Who can count the dust of Jacob"?

172.   Who said, "Let me die the death of the righteous, and may my final end be like theirs"?

173. What is the name of the field on the top of Pisgah?

174. Who has the strength of a wild ox?

175. Who said, "There is no divination against Jacob, no evil omens against Israel"?

176. Who was summoned to curse the Israelites but blessed them instead?

177. Name the man who self-witnessed, "I have the knowledge from the Most High."

178. Who said, "A star will come out of Jacob; a scepter will rise out of Israel"?

179. Who was first among the nations?

180. Name the place where the Israelite men began to indulge in sexual immorality with Moabite women.

181. Who killed the Israelite man and the Midianite woman who were indulged in sexual immorality?

182. How many Israelites died in the plague at Shittim when the Lord's anger rose against them?

183. Who turned away the Lord's anger from the Israelites and who was zealous for the Lord's honor among the Israelites?

184. Name the man with whom the Lord made his covenant of Peace.

185. What was the name of the Israelite man who was killed by Phinehas at Shittim?

186. What was the name of the Midianite woman who was killed by Phinehas at Shittim?

187. What was the name of the tribal chief of the Midianite family and the father of Kozbi, a Midianite woman who was killed because of her sexual immorality?

188. When Moses took his second census, how did the number compare to the first census?

189. Name the sons of Judah who died in Canaan.

190. Name the daughters of Zelphehad.

191. Who was the daughter of Asher?

192. Who was the forefather of Amram?

193. Who were the parents of Moses and Aaron?

194. Who was the sister of Moses and Aaron?

195. Who was the father of Gilead?

196. Who was the son of Gilead and father of Zelophehad?

197. Whose daughters received an inheritance in the property among their father's relatives?

198. From which mountain did Moses see the land of Canaan?

199. Name the man who was appointed by the Lord as the successor of Moses.

200. Which was the offering that included wine?

201. Who can disallow the vow of a married woman when he hears of it?

202. At the time of Moses, how many men from each tribe of Israel went for war with the Midianites?

203. How did Balaam die?

204. At the time of Moses, when the Israelites sought revenge from the Midianites, how many virgins were captured by the Israelite soldiers?

205. Who remained loyal to the Lord?

206. Who were made to wander in the wilderness by the Lord?

207. Which tribes were given land east of Jordan?

208. Which cities' names were changed by the Reuben tribes?

209. Who invaded the land of Gilead and drove out the Amorites?

210. To whom did Moses give the land of Gilead?

211. Who attacked and captured a city and renamed it after himself?

212. What was the old name of the Nobah city?

213. What is the other name for the wilderness of Zin?

214. Name the mountain where Aaron died?

215. At what age did Aaron die?

216. Who set the boundaries of the land of Canaan for the Israelites?

217. How many towns in total were to be given to the Levites?

218. How many towns were to be selected as cities of refuge?

219. How many refugee cities were there in the east of Jordan?

220. How many refugee cities were there in the land of Canaan?

221. What type of murderer was allowed to go to a city of refuge?

222. How many witnesses were required before a man was put to death?

223. Why must a daughter who inherits land marry within their own tribe?

Who said to whom?

224. "Wait until I find out what the Lord commands concerning you."

225. "Come with us and we will treat you well, for the Lord has promised good things to Israel."

226. "I will not go; I am going back to my own land and my own people."

227. "Please do not leave us. You know where we should camp in the wilderness, and you can be our eyes."

228. "If you come with us, we will share with you whatever good things the Lord gives us."

229. "Why should you ask me to act like a nurse and carry them in my arms like babies?"

230. "I cannot carry all these people by myself; the burden is too heavy for me."

231. "If this is how you are going to treat me, please go ahead and kill me."

232. "Are you jealous for my sake?"

233. "When there are prophets among you, I reveal myself to them in visions and speak to them in dreams."

234. "Please, my lord, I ask you not to hold against us the sin we have so foolishly committed."

235. "Do not rebel against the Lord."

236. "Now may the Lord's strength be displayed."

237. "In the morning the Lord will show who belongs to him and who is holy."

238. "Will you be angry with the entire assembly when only one man sins?"

239. "This horde is going to lick up everything around us, as an ox licks up the grass of the field."

240. "A people have come out of Egypt; they cover the face of the land."

241. "Come and put a curse on these people."

242. "I know that whoever you bless is blessed and whoever you curse is cursed."

243. "Who are these men with you?"

244. "Do not go with them. You must not put a curse on those people."

245. "Go back to your own country, for the Lord has refused to let me go with you."

246. "I will reward you handsomely and do whatever you say."

247. "If only I had a sword in my hand, I would kill you right now."

248. "I have come here to oppose you."

249. "Your path is a reckless one before me."

250. "I have sinned. I did not realize you were standing in the road to oppose me."

251. "Am I really not able to reward you?"

252. "Well, I have come to you now. But I can't say whatever I please."

253. "Build me seven altars here, and prepare seven bulls and seven rams for me."

254. "Stay here beside your offering while I go aside."

255. "How can I curse those whom God has not cursed? How can I denounce those whom the Lord has not denounced?"

256. "What have you done to me? I brought you to curse my enemies, but you have done nothing but bless them."

257. "Must I not speak what the Lord puts in my mouth?"

258. "God is not human, that he should lie, not a human being, that he should change his mind."

259. "I have received a command to bless."

260. "Neither curse them at all nor bless them at all."

261. "Did I not tell you I must do whatever the Lord says?"

262. "Now leave at once and go home."

263. "I said I would reward you handsomely, but the Lord has kept you from being rewarded."

264. "Now I am going back to my people."

265. "Come; let me warn you of what this people will do to your people in days to come."

266. "Our father died in the wilderness. He was not among Korah's followers, who banded together against the Lord."

267. "He died for his own sin and left no sons."

268. "Why should our father's name disappear from his clan because he had no son?"

Deuteronomy

Deuteronomy

The genre of the book of Deuteronomy is not much different from that of Exodus. It is a Narrative History and Law, although there is a Song from Moses just after he commissioned Joshua. This song describes the History that the Israelites had experienced. Moses wrote Deuteronomy at approximately 1407 -1406 B.C. The key personalities are Moses and Joshua.

Moses wrote this book to remind the Israelites of what God had done and to remind them of what God expects of them. The name literally means *"Second Law"*. Moses gives *"the Law"* for the second time.

• Chapters 1-4, Moses reviews some of the details of the past history of Israel such as the Exodus and the wandering in the wilderness. He then urges that they obey the Laws of God.

• Chapters 5-28, Moses restates the Ten Commandments to the Israelites. Moses explains the principles and instructions for living a godly life as God's chosen nation. These include how to love the Lord, laws of worship, laws regarding relationships (like divorce), and also the consequences and penalties if these laws are broken.

• Chapters 29-30 there is a move to commit themselves, as a nation, and to stand apart unto God. This consists of not only knowing the many laws that God has commanded, but also obeying them and placing God first.

Finally, in chapters 31-34, we see the first change in leadership in Israel. Moses the one who has been leading them the entire time, hands over his authority to Joshua, and commissions him. Moses blesses the tribes, which reminds us of Jacob blessing his sons almost 450 years earlier. In the last chapter, God shows Moses the Promised Land, although he cannot enter it. After this, Moses the servant of the Lord dies on Mt. Nebo.

1. How many chapters are there in this book?

2. How many verses are there in this book?

3. Who is the author of this book?

4. When was this book written?

5. How many days does it take to go from Horeb to Kadesh Barnea by the Mount Seir road?

6. Name the Amorite king who reigned in Heshbon.

7. Where did the king of Bashan reign?

8. Who was the king of Bashan?

9. Where did the Israelites defeat King Sihon and King Og?

10. Upto which great river did the Lord ask the Israelites to go?

11. How far did the Israelites explore the land of Canaan?

12. Why were the Israelites not able to enter the Promised Land after sending out the spies?

13. The book of Deuteronomy mentions a man who followed the Lord wholeheartedly. Who is he?

14. What was Moses to do for Joshua?

15. Who chased the Israelites like a swarm of bees?

16. To whom did the Lord give the hill country of Seir?

17. From whom did the Israelites purchase their food and water?

18. The land belonging to whose descendants were the Israelites not to possess?

19. Who lived in Ar–a people strong and numerous and as tall as Anakites?

20.   What did the Moabites call the Rephaites who lived in Ar?

21.   Who did the descendants of Esau drive out of Seir?

22.   How many years had passed from the time the Israelites left Kadesh Barnea until they crossed the Zerod Valley?

23.   What did the Ammonites call the Rephaites who lived in Ar?

24.   From where did Moses send messengers to Sihon king of Heshbon offering him peace?

25.   In which region did king Og of Bashan have his kingdom with 60 cities?

26.   The cities of which kingdom were fortified with high walls, gates and bars?

27.   What did the Sidonians call Mount Hermon as?

28.   What did the Amorites call Mount Hermon as?

29.   Whose bed was decorated with iron?

30.   What was the dimension of Og's bed?

31.   Where was the bed of Og, king of Bashan when the book of Deuteronomy was written?

32.   Which region is known as the land of Rephaites?

33.   Who named Bashan as HavvothJair?

34.   By what other name is the sea of the Arabah also known as?

35.   From where was Moses able to see the land beyond Jordan?

36.   What were the Israelites forbidden from doing to the Lord's commandments?

37. Which nation is compared as the iron smelting furnace?

38. What did the Lord warn Israel would happen if they made idols?

39. Who heard the voice of the Lord out of the darkness, while the mountain was ablaze with fire?

40. What should we teach our children?

41. When should the Israelites be careful not to forget God?

42. What were the Israelites to do to the nations that dwelled in the land of Canaan?

43. Who was tested for 40 years?

44. For how many years did the clothes of the Israelites not wear out?

45. Whom did the Lord discipline just as a man disciplines his son?

46. Name the land where the rocks are iron and one can dig copper out of the hills?

47. What power did the Lord give to the Israelites?

48. The people of which nation were strong and tall?

49. What was inscribed by the finger of God?

50. Name the places where the Israelites made the Lord angry.

51. Who laid prostrate before the Lord for 40 days and 40 nights?

52. Whose prayer prevented the Lord from destroying Israel?

53. Where did Moses put the second set of the Ten Commandments?

54. According to the book of Deuteronomy, where did Aaron die?

55. After the death of Aaron, who succeeded him as a priest?

56. Whom did the Lord not destroy after hearing the plea of Moses?

57. Which river was mentioned describing the extent of the land to be given to the Israelites?

58. What was to be done to a relative that tried to get the Israelite to follow other gods?

59. What had God chosen Israel to be?

60. How would a person tithe who lived a long way from the place where the Lord chose?

61. What were the Israelites to do with the tithes every third year?

62. What was Israel to do to nations with regard to money?

63. What was to be done to a servant who did not wish to be released?

64. What were the Israelites forbidden to do with an animal that is crippled or blind?

65. Why did Israel desire a king?

66. Who would the Prophet that the Lord was going to raise up be like?

67. What were the Israelites not to remove?

68. How many witnesses were required to convict anyone accused of any crime or offence they may have committed?

69. What did the Israelites have to offer when they went to a city for a fight?

70. How much was the inheritance of the firstborn son compared to the others?

71. How long was the body of a cursed man allowed to hang on a tree?

72. What was a person to do with an animal or item they had found?

73. What was a person not to wear?

74. Whose descendants, even the tenth generation was not allowed to enter the assembly of the Lord?

75. Name the hometown of Balaam.

76. Who was the father of Balaam?

77. What sanitation rule was given to the Israelites?

78. Whose earnings were not allowed in the house of the Lord as a pay to any vow?

79. What were the Israelites allowed to eat from their neighbor's land?

80. How long after the marriage was a man free not to go to war?

81. How often did the Israelites have to pay a servant who was poor?

82. What was the maximum number of blows a man could receive during a beating?

83. What were the Israelites to do to the Amalekites?

84. Where did the Israelites set up stones coated with plaster?

85. After crossing the Jordan River, where did the Israelites set up the stones with the commandments of the Lord?

86.   After crossing the Jordan River, from which mountain were the blessings pronounced from?

87.   After crossing the Jordan River, from which mountain were the curses pronounced?

88.   Which tribes stood on Mount Gerizim?

89.   Which tribes stood on Mount Ebal?

90.   To whom did Moses deliver the law?

91.   From which mountain did Moses see the land of Canaan?

92.   In which mountain range is Mount Nebo?

93.   Who will live like a lion, tearing at arm or head?

94.   Who is most blessed of sons?

95.   Which city is known as the City of Palms?

96.   Where did Moses die?

97.   Where did the Lord bury Moses?

98.   How old was Moses when he died?

99.   Name the prophet whose eyes weren't weak or his strength gone until his death?

100.   Where did the Israelites grieve for Moses?

101.   For how many days did the Israelites grieve for Moses?

102.   Name the man who was filled with the spirit of wisdom for Moses had laid his hands on him.

Who said to whom?

103.   "What you propose to do is good."

104.   "Do not be afraid; do not be discouraged."

105. "We have sinned against the Lord."

106. "Today we have seen that a person can live even if God speaks with them."

107. "We will die if we hear the voice of the Lord our God any longer."

108. "I have heard what this people said to you. Everything they said was good."

109. "Go; tell them to return to their tents."

110. "You stay here with me."

111. "The Lord – and the Lord alone – is our God."

112. "Go down from here at once."

113. "I have seen this people, and they are stiff-necked people indeed!"

114. "You have been rebellious against the Lord ever since I have known you."

115. "The Lord himself goes before you and will be with you; he will never leave you nor forsake you."

116. "If you have been rebellious against the Lord while I am still alive and with you, how much more will you rebel after I die!"

Answers

Genesis

1. 50 chapters
2. 1533 verses
3. Moses
4. 1400 B.C.
5. It was formless and desolate (1:1-2)
6. Over the water (1:2)
7. Light (1:3)
8. Light (1:4)
9. Day (1:5)
10. Night (1:5)
11. Sky (1:6-7)
12. Land and sea (1:9-10)
13. Earth (1:9-10)
14. Sea (1:10)
15. Third day (1:11-13)
16. Sun, moon and stars (1:14-16)
17. Sun (1:14-16)
18. Moon and stars (1:14-16)
19. Birds and aquatic creatures (1:20-23)
20. To reproduce and fill the sea and the sky (1:20-23)
21. Animals and human beings (1:24-31)
22. They looked like God and resembled them (1:24-31)
23. Human beings (1:24-31)
24. Six days (1:1-31)
25. 3rd and 6th day (1:10-12; 25-31)
26. Seventh day (2:3)

27.	East (2:8)
28.	Tree of life and tree of knowledge (2:9)
29.	Pishon, Gihon, Tigris and Euphrates (2:10-14)
30.	Pishon (2:11)
31.	Havilah (2:11-12)
32.	Gihon (2:13)
33.	Tigris (2:14)
34.	Fruit from the tree of knowledge (2:16-17)
35.	Man (2:20)
36.	Adam (2:21)
37.	Rib (2:21)
38.	Snake (3:1)
39.	Snake (3:1)
40.	Snake (3:4)
41.	Fig leaves (3:7)
42.	Snake (3:14)
43.	It would crush the serpent's head (3:15)
44.	Eve (3:20)
45.	Cherubim (3:24)
46.	Cain (4:1)
47.	Farmer (4:2)
48.	Shepherd (4:2)
49.	Cain (4:5)
50.	Cain (4:8)
51.	Cain (4:9)
52.	Mark given by God to Cain (4:15)
53.	Land of Nod (4:16)
54.	Enoch (4:17)

55. Cain; Enoch (4:17)
56. Rad (4:18)
57. Lamech (4:19)
58. Adah and Zillah (4:19)
59. Jabal (4:20)
60. Jubal (4:21)
61. Tubal Cain (4:22)
62. Naamah (4:22)
63. Zillah (4:22)
64. 77 (4:24)
65. Seth (4:25)
66. Enosh (4:26)
67. Enosh (4:26)
68. 30 (5:3)
69. 800 (5:4)
70. 930 (5:5)
71. 105 (5:6)
72. 912 (5:8)
73. 90 (5:9)
74. 905 (5:11)
75. 70 (5:12)
76. 910 (5:14)
77. 65 (5:15)
78. 895 (5:17)
79. 162 (5:18)
80. 962 (5:20)
81. 65 (5:21)
82. God took him (5:24)

83.   365 (5:21-24)
84.   187 (5:25)
85.   969 (5:27)
86.   Methuselah (5:27)
87.   182 (5:28)
88.   777 (5:31)
89.   500 (5:32)
90.   Shem, Ham and Japheth (5:32)
91.   From the time of Noah (6:3)
92.   Noah (6:7)
93.   Noah (6:9)
94.   Gopher/Timber (6:14)
95.   Tar/Pitch (6:14)
96.   300 cubits long, 50 cubits wide and 30 cubits high (6:15)
97.   01 (6:16)
98.   7 pairs (7:2)
99.   1 pair (7:2)
100. 600 (7:6)
101. 7 days (7:10)
102. 40 days (7:12)
103. God (7:16)
104. 15 cubits (7:20)
105. 150 days (7:24)
106. Ararat (8:4)
107. On the 17th day of the 7th month (8:4)
108. On the 1st day of the 10th month (8:5)
109. Raven (8:7)
110. Raven and Dove (8:7,11)

111. By the 1st day of the 1st month and 27th day of the 2nd month of Noah's 601st year (8:13-14)
112. Noah (8:20)
113. Noah (9:3)
114. Rainbow (9:12-13)
115. Ham (9:18)
116. Farmer (9:20)
117. Noah (9:20)
118. Noah (9:21)
119. Noah (9:21)
120. Shem and Japheth (9:23)
121. Ham (9:25)
122. Ham (9:25)
123. 350 (9:28)
124. 950 (9:28)
125. Cush (10:8)
126. A mighty hunter (10:8-9)
127. Nimrod (10:8-9)
128. Resen (10:12)
129. Resen (10:12)
130. Peleg (10:25)
131. Joktan (10:25)
132. Babel (11:8-9)
133. Arpachshad (11:10)
134. Nahor (11:24)
135. 29 (11:24)
136. Terah (11:26)
137. Nahor and Haran (11:26)

138. Haran (11:27)
139. Sarai (11:29)
140. Milcah (11:29)
141. Milcah (11:29)
142. Haran (11:31)
143. Haran (11:31-32)
144. 205 (11:32)
145. Abram (12:2)
146. 75 (12:4)
147. Shechem (12:6)
148. Abram (12:7)
149. Sarai (12:14)
150. Sarai (12:16)
151. Sarai (12:15; 20:7)
152. Sodom and Gomorrah (13:10)
153. Lot (13:12)
154. Sodom (13:13)
155. Near the great trees of Mamre (13:18)
156. Bala (14:2)
157. Valley of Siddim (14:3)
158. Mishpat (14:7)
159. Valley of Siddim (14:9)
160. 9 (14:9)
161. Valley of Siddim (14:10)
162. Bera and Birsha (14:2; 10)
163. Genesis (14:13)
164. 318 (14:14)
165. Valley of Shaveh (14:17)

Answers – Genesis

166. Valley of Shaveh (14:17)
167. Melchizedek (14:18)
168. Melchizedek (14:18)
169. King Melchizedek (14:20)
170. Abram (14:20)
171. King of Sodom (14:22)
172. Aner, Eshkol and Mamre (14:24)
173. Eliezer (15:2)
174. Abram (15:12)
175. 400 years (15:13)
176. River Euphrates (15:18)
177. Kenites, Kenizzites, Kadmonites, Hittites, Perizzites, Rephaim, Amorites, Canaanites, Grigashites and Jebusites (15:19-21)
178. Sarai (16:1)
179. Hagar (16:1)
180. Hagar (16:4)
181. Hagar (16:6)
182. A spring in the desert on the road to Shur (16:7)
183. Ishmael (16:12)
184. Ishmael (16:12)
185. Beer LahaiRoi (16:14)
186. 86 years (16:16)
187. 99 years (17:1)
188. Abraham (17:5)
189. To circumcise every male child (17:9-11)
190. 8 days (17:11-12)
191. Sarah (17:15-16)
192. Ishmael (17:20)

193.	99 years (17:24)
194.	13 years (17:25)
195.	Abraham and Ishmael (17:26)
196.	Abraham (18:4, 8)
197.	Sarah (18:12)
198.	Sarah (18:15)
199.	Abraham (18:23)
200.	Abraham (18:27)
201.	6 times (18:22-33)
202.	50, 45, 40, 30, 20 and 10 (18:22-33)
203.	At the city gate (19:1)
204.	The angels who came to destroy Sodom (19:3)
205.	Lot (19:3)
206.	Lot (19:4)
207.	Sodom (19:11)
208.	Zoar (19:23)
209.	Burning sulphur (19:24)
210.	Lot's wife (19:26)
211.	Lot's daughters (19:30)
212.	Lot's daughters (19:32-35)
213.	Lot's daughters (19:32-35)
214.	Moab (19:37)
215.	Benammi (19:38)
216.	Abimelech (20:2-3)
217.	Abimelech (20:4)
218.	Abraham (20:11-12)
219.	Abimelech (20:14)
220.	1000 (20:16)

221.   Sarah (20:17-18)
222.   Abraham (20:7; 17)
223.   100 years (21:4)
224.   Sarah (21:6)
225.   Abraham (21:8)
226.   Hagar (21:14)
227.   Ishmael (21:20-21)
228.   Phicol (21:22)
229.   About a well seized by Abimelech's servant (21:25)
230.   Abimelech (21:27)
231.   7 ewe lambs (21:28-30)
232.   Beersheba (21:31)
233.   Tamarisk tree (21:33)
234.   Offer him as a burnt offering (22:2)
235.   Moriah (22:2)
236.   2 servants (22:3)
237.   3 days (22:4)
238.   Ram (22:13)
239.   The Lord Provides (22:14)
240.   Uz (22:20)
241.   127 (23:1)
242.   KiriathArba (Hebron) (23:2)
243.   Abraham (23:9)
244.   Ephron son of Zohar (23:7)
245.   400 (23:16)
246.   Machpelah (23:17)
247.   Abraham's servant (24:12)
248.   Bethuel (24:15)

249. Rebecca (24:16)
250. A beka (24:22)
251. 10 Shekels (24:22)
252. Nahor (24:24)
253. Milcah (24:24)
254. Laban (24:29)
255. Isaac (24:62-63)
256. Beer LahaiRoi (24:62-65)
257. Keturah (25:1)
258. 175 (25:7)
259. Nebaioth (25:12-13)
260. 137 (25:17)
261. Descendants of Ishmael (25:18)
262. 40 years (25:20)
263. Isaac (25:21)
264. Esau (25:25)
265. Esau (25:25)
266. Jacob (25:26)
267. 60 years (25:26)
268. Esau (25:27)
269. Jacob (25:27)
270. Edom (25:30)
271. Esau (25:32-33)
272. Esau (25:34)
273. Gerar (26:1-2)
274. Isaac (26:1-4)
275. Isaac (26:12)
276. Isaac (26:13)

277. Philistines (26:15)
278. Esek and Sitnah (26:20-21)
279. Rehoboth (26:22)
280. Ahuzzath (26:26)
281. Shibah (26:33)
282. 40 years (26:34)
283. Judith, Basemath and Mahalath (26:34; 28:9)
284. Isaac and Rebecca (26:34-35)
285. Jacob put on Esau's clothes and goat skins on his hands and neck (27:15-17)
286. Jacob (27:36)
287. Esau (27:38)
288. Esau (27:40)
289. Kill him (27:41)
290. Mahalath (28:9)
291. Jacob (28:12)
292. Jacob (28:16)
293. Bethel (28:17-19)
294. Jacob (28:18-19)
295. Luz (28:19)
296. Jacob (28:19)
297. Bethel (28:19-20)
298. Jacob (28:22)
299. Jacob (29:11)
300. 1 month (29:14)
301. Leah and Rachel (29:16)
302. Leah (29:17)
303. Rachel (29:17)

304. Rachel (29:18)
305. Zilpah (29:24)
306. Bilhah (29:28)
307. 14 years (29:20-30)
308. Reuben (29:32)
309. Levi (29:32-35)
310. Rachel (30:8)
311. Leah (30:13)
312. Leah (30:16)
313. Dinah (30:21)
314. Joseph (30:24)
315. Jacob (30:30)
316. Speckled and spotted livestock (30:32)
317. Poplar, almond and plane tree (30:37)
318. Laban (31:7)
319. Jacob (31:13)
320. Rachel (31:19)
321. 7 Days (31:23)
322. In the hill country of Gilead (31:23-25)
323. Genesis (31:27)
324. Rachel (31:35)
325. 6 years (31:41)
326. Jacob (31:40)
327. 20 years (31:41)
328. Jacob (31:41)
329. JegarSahadutha (31:47)
330. Galeed (31:47)
331. Covenant memorial set up by Jacob and Laban (31:46-48)

332.   Mizpah (31:49)
333.   Laban (31:55)
334.   Jacob (32:2)
335.   Mahanaim (32:2)
336.   Land of Seir (32:3)
337.   400 men (32:6)
338.   Jacob (32:10)
339.   200 (32:14)
340.   220 goats and 220 rams (32:14)
341.   30 (32:15)
342.   40 cows and 10 bulls (32:15)
343.   10 male and 20 female donkeys (32:15)
344.   Jacob (32:20)
345.   Jabbok River (32:22)
346.   Jacob (32:28)
347.   Israel (32:28)
348.   Jacob (32:30)
349.   Peniel (32:30)
350.   Hip out of joint (32:25, 31-32)
351.   Jacob (33:3)
352.   Jacob and Esau (33:4)
353.   Jacob (33:10)
354.   Esau (33:11)
355.   Sukkoth (33:17)
356.   Hamor (33:19)
357.   100 pieces (33:19)
358.   El Elohe Israel (33:20)
359.   Leah (34:1)

360. Shechem (34:2)
361. Shechem (34:3)
362. Jacob (34:5)
363. Shechem (34:2, 19)
364. He should be circumcised (34:15-16)
365. Simeon and Levi (34:25)
366. Sons of Jacob (34:27)
367. Bethel (35:1)
368. Put away the foreign gods that are among you (35:2)
369. Under the oak at Shechem (35:4)
370. El Bethel (35:7)
371. Deborah (35:8)
372. Under the oak outside Bethel (35:8)
373. AllonBakuth (35:8)
374. Jacob (35:14-15)
375. Jacob (35:18)
376. Ben-Oni (35:18)
377. Some distance from Ephrath (35:16-18)
378. Ephrath (35:19)
379. Jacob (35:20)
380. Reuben (35:22)
381. Bilhah (35:22)
382. KiriathArba (35:27)
383. 180 years (35:28)
384. Reuben, Simeon, Levi, Judah, Issachar, Zebulun, Joseph, Benjamin, Dan, Naphtali, Gad and Asher (35:22-26)
385. Reuben, Simeon, Levi, Judah, Issachar and Zebulun (35:23)

Answers – Genesis

386. Joseph and Benjamin (35:24)
387. Dan and Naphtali (35:25)
388. Gad and Asher (35:26)
389. Edom (36:1)
390. Basemath (36:1-3)
391. Esau and Jacob (36:6-7)
392. Esau (36:8)
393. Esau (36:9)
394. Anah (36:24)
395. Zibeon (36:24)
396. Oholibamah (36:25)
397. Bela (36:32)
398. Dinhabah (36:32)
399. Hadad (36:35)
400. Avith (36:35)
401. Pau (36:39)
402. Mehetabel (36:39)
403. 17 years (37:2)
404. Joseph (37:3)
405. Joseph (37:3)
406. Joseph (37:4)
407. Joseph (37:11)
408. Dothan (37:17)
409. Reuben (37:21)
410. Judah (37:26)
411. 20 (37:28)
412. Reuben (37:29)
413. Jacob (37:34)

414. Jacob (37:35)
415. Potiphar (37:36)
416. One of the Pharaoh's officials, the captain of the guard (37:36)
417. Hirah (38:1)
418. Er (38:3)
419. Onan and Shelah (38:4-5)
420. Kezib (38:5)
421. Tamar (38:6)
422. Er (38:7)
423. Tamar (38:11)
424. At the entrance of Enaim (38:14)
425. Tamar (38:17-18)
426. His seal, cord and staff (38:25)
427. Perez and Zerah (38:30)
428. Zerah (38:30)
429. Joseph (39:6)
430. Potiphar's wife (39:7)
431. His cloak (39:13)
432. Attempted rape (39:14)
433. In charge of all the prisoners (39:22)
434. Chief Cupbearer and Chief Baker (40:2-7)
435. 3 days (40:12; 18)
436. Cupbearer (40:21)
437. 2 years (41:1)
438. 14 (41:1-4)
439. Pharaoh's (41:8)
440. Joseph (41:14)

441. Seven years of plenty followed by seven years of famine (41:29-30)
442. Over all the land of Egypt, second only to Pharaoh (41:40-41)
443. Joseph (41:42)
444. Joseph (41:42)
445. Zaphenath – Paneah (41:45)
446. Asenath (41:45)
447. Pothiphera, priest of On (41:45)
448. 30 years (41:46)
449. 13 years {30-17=13} (37:2; 41:46)
450. Joseph (41:49)
451. Manasseh (41:51)
452. Ephraim (41:52)
453. 10 (42:3)
454. Benjamin (42:4)
455. Joseph (42:7)
456. To bring their youngest brother (42:15)
457. 3 days (42:17)
458. Joseph (42:23)
459. Simeon (42:24)
460. Jacob sons (42:36)
461. Jacob (42:36)
462. Honey, balm, spices, myrrh, pistachio nuts and almonds (43:11)
463. Joseph (43:30)
464. Benjamin (43:34)
465. He would be a slave (44:10)
466. Benjamin (44:12)

467. Jacobs' sons (44:13)
468. Jacob and Benjamin (44:22)
469. Judah (44:32)
470. Joseph's brothers (45:3)
471. To save the lives of the descendants of Jacob (45:5, 7)
472. 5 years (45:6)
473. 2 years (45:6)
474. 5 sets of clothes and 300 shekels of silver (45:22)
475. Jacob (45:26)
476. When he saw the carts Joseph had sent (45:26-28)
477. Beersheba (46:1)
478. Er and Onan (46:12)
479. 10 (46:21)
480. 70 (46:27)
481. Goshen (46:29)
482. Goshen (46:34)
483. 5 brothers (47:2)
484. Shepherds (47:3)
485. Jacob (47:8)
486. 130 years (47:9)
487. Rameses (47:11)
488. Land of the Priests (47:22)
489. Priests (47:22)
490. 17 years (47:28)
491. 147 years (47:28)
492. Manasseh (48:14)
493. Jacob (48:20)

494.   Joseph (48:22)
495.   Reuben (49:4)
496.   Reuben (49:4)
497.   Simeon and Levi (49:5)
498.   Simeon and Levi (49:5)
499.   Judah (49:8)
500.   Judah (49:9)
501.   Judah (49:10)
502.   Judah (49:11)
503.   Judah (49:12)
504.   Zebulun (49:13)
505.   Issachar (49:14)
506.   Dan (49:17)
507.   Dan (49:17)
508.   Gad (49:19)
509.   Asher (49:20)
510.   Naphtali (49:21)
511.   Joseph (49:22)
512.   Joseph (49:23)
513.   Joseph (49:24)
514.   Benjamin (49:27)
515.   Benjamin (49:27)
516.   Sarah, Rebecca and Leah (49:31)
517.   Joseph (50:1)
518.   40 days (50:3)
519.   70 days (50:3)
520.   Atad (50:10)
521.   7 days (50:10)

522.   Abel Mizraim (50:11)
523.   Abel Mizraim (50:11)
524.   110 years (50:22)
525.   Makir (50:23)
526.   That they would carry his bones out of Egypt (50:25)
527.   Joseph's (50:26)

Who said to whom?
528.   Lord to Cain (4:6)
529.   Lord to Cain (4:7)
530.   Cain to Lord (4:9)
531.   Lord to Cain (4:12)
532.   Cain to Lord (4:14)
533.   Cain to Lord (4:14)
534.   Lord to Noah (7:1)
535.   Lord to Abram (12:3)
536.   Pharaoh to Abram (12:19)
537.   Abraham to Lot (13:8)
538.   Abram to Lot (13:9)
539.   Bera the King of Sodom to Abram (14:21)
540.   Lord to Abram (15:15)
541.   Sarai to Abram (16:5)
542.   Abram to Sarai (16:6)
543.   Angel of the Lord to Hagar (16:8)
544.   Angel of the Lord to Hagar (16:9)
545.   Hagar to the Angel of the Lord (16:13)
546.   Abraham to the three angels of the Lord (18:3)
547.   Abraham to the three angels of the Lord (18:5)
548.   Lord to Abraham (18:14)

549. Lot to the men of Sodom (19:8)
550. The men of Sodom to Lot (19:9)
551. Angels of the Lord to Lot (19:12)
552. Lot to his sons-in-law, who were pledged to marry his daughters (19:14)
553. Angels of the Lord to Lot (19:17)
554. Angels of the Lord to Lot (19:17)
555. Lot to the Angels of the Lord (19:19)
556. Angels of the Lord to Lot (19:22)
557. Abimelek to the Lord (20:5)
558. Lord to Abimelek (20:6)
559. Lord to Abimelek (20:7)
560. Abhimelek to Abraham (20:9)
561. Abhimelek to Abraham (20:9)
562. Abhimelek to Abraham (20:10)
563. Abraham to Abhimelek (20:12)
564. Abhimelek to Abraham (20:15)
565. God to Hagar (21:17)
566. Abhimelek to Abraham (21:22)
567. Abraham to Hittites (23:4)
568. Hittites to Abraham (23:5)
569. Ephron to Abraham (23:15)
570. Abraham to his servant (24:6)
571. Abraham's servant to Rebecca (24:17)
572. Laban to the servants of Abraham (24:31)
573. Abraham's servant to Laban (24:33)
574. Laban and Bethuel to Abraham's servant (24:50)

575. Abraham's servant to Laban and Bethuel (24:56)
576. Laban and his mother to Rebecca (24:60)
577. Isaac to Abhimelek, Ahuzzath and Phicol (26:26-27)
578. Isaac to Esau (27:2)
579. Rebecca to Jacob (27:8)
580. Rebecca to Jacob (27:13)
581. Isaac to Jacob (27:26)
582. Esau to Isaac (27:36)
583. Isaac to Esau (27:37)
584. Esau to Isaac (27:38)
585. Rebecca to Jacob (27:45)
586. Laban to Jacob (29:14)
587. Laban to Jacob (29:15)
588. Laban to Jacob (29:19)
589. Jacob to Laban (29:25)
590. Laban to Jacob (29:26)
591. Rachel to Jacob (30:1)
592. Jacob to Rachel (30:2)
593. Jacob to Laban (30:25)
594. Jacob to Laban (30:26)
595. Laban to Jacob (30:27)
596. Laban to Jacob (30:28)
597. Jacob to Laban (30:30)
598. Jacob to Laban (30:30)
599. Jacob to Laban (30:31)
600. Lord to Jacob (31:3)
601. Leah and Rachel to Jacob (31:14)
602. Laban to Jacob (31:28)

603.   Laban to Jacob (31:29)
604.   Rachel to Laban (31:35)
605.   Jacob to Laban (31:36)
606.   Laban to Jacob (31:43)
607.   Laban to Jacob (31:49)
608.   Laban to Jacob (31:51)
609.   Lord to Jacob (32:26)
610.   Jacob to Lord (32:26)
611.   Lord to Jacob (32:29)
612.   Esau to Jacob (33:9)
613.   Jacob to Esau (33:10)
614.   Jacob to Esau (33:11)
615.   Esau to Jacob (33:12)
616.   Hamor to Jacob and his sons (34:10)
617.   Shechem to Jacob and his sons (34:12)
618.   Hamor and Shechem to the men of the city (34:21)
619.   Jacob to Simeon and Levi (34:30)
620.   Jacob to Joseph (37:13)
621.   Judah to his brothers (37:27)
622.   Judah to Tamar (38:16)
623.   Tamar to Judah (38:16)
624.   Judah to Hirah his friend (38:23)
625.   Joseph to Potiphar's wife (39:9)
626.   Joseph to Potiphar's wife (39:9)
627.   The cupbearer and the baker to Joseph (40:8)
628.   Joseph to the cupbearer and the baker (40:8)
629.   Chief cupbearer to the Pharaoh (41:9)
630.   Pharaoh to his official (41:38)

631. Pharaoh to Joseph (41:40)
632. Jacob to his sons (42:1)
633. Joseph to his brothers (42:9)
634. Jacob's sons to Joseph (42:11)
635. Jacob to his sons (42:36)
636. Jacob to his sons (42:38)
637. Judah to Jacob (43:10)
638. Jacob to his sons (43:14)
639. Joseph to Benjamin (43:29)
640. Steward to the brothers of Joseph (44:4)
641. Joseph's brothers to steward (44:7)
642. Judah to Joseph (44:16)
643. Judah to Joseph (44:34)
644. Joseph to his attendants (45:1)
645. Pharaoh to Joseph (45:18)
646. Pharaoh to Joseph (45:20)
647. Joseph to his brothers (45:24)
648. Lord to Jacob (46:3)
649. Jacob to Pharaoh (47:9)
650. People to Joseph (47:25)
651. Jacob to Joseph (48:19)
652. Jacob to Joseph (48:21)
653. Jacob to his sons (49:1)
654. Joseph's brothers to Joseph (50:17)
655. Joseph to his brothers (50:19)
656. Joseph to his brothers (50:20)
657. Joseph to his brothers (50:21)
658. Joseph to the Israelites (50:25)

Exodus

1. 40 chapters
2. 1213 verses
3. Moses
4. 1450-1410 B.C.
5. Reuben, Simeon, Levi, Judah, Issachar, Zebulun, Benjamin, Dan, Joseph, Naphtali, Gad and Asher. (1:1-3)
6. 70 (1:5)
7. Israelites (1:11)
8. Pithom and Rameses (1:11)
9. Israelites (1:12)
10. Shiphrah and Puah (1:15)
11. Kill all the boy babies (1:15-16)
12. Hebrew women (1:19)
13. The families of their own (Ex. 1:21)
14. Levi (2:1)
15. 3 months (2:2)
16. Miriam (2:4)
17. Moses' mother (2:9)
18. Pharaoh's daughter (2:10)
19. Moses (2:10)
20. An Egyptian (2:11-12)
21. Midian (2:15-16)
22. 7 (2:16; 3:1)
23. He was a priest of Midian. (2:16; 3:1)
24. Zipporah (2:21; 3:1)
25. Gershom (2:22)
26. Moses (2:22)

27. Jethro (2:21; 3:1)
28. Mount Horeb/Sinai (3:1)
29. Burning bush (3:1-3)
30. Moses (3:2)
31. Moses (3:6)
32. Moses (3:13)
33. I AM (3:14)
34. 3 days (3:18)
35. Egyptians (3:22; 12:36)
36. A walking stick (4:2)
37. 3(4:1-9)
38. Moses (4:10)
39. Aaron (4:16)
40. Levi (4:14)
41. Moses (4:16)
42. A walking stick/Staff (4:17)
43. Zipporah (4:20)
44. Moses (4:24)
45. Zipporah (4:25)
46. Zipporah (4:26)
47. Aaron (4:27)
48. Pharaoh, the king of Egypt (5:1)
49. To allow them to travel 3 days into the desert to offer sacrifices and to worship the Lord. (5:3)
50. Stubble (5:12)
51. Egyptian slave drivers (5:13)
52. Make the Israelites produce same number of bricks without providing straw (5:6-13)
53. To Abraham, Isaac and Jacob (6:3)

54.   To Abraham, Isaac and Jacob (6:4)
55.   Israelites (6:9)
56.   Moses (6:8)
57.   4 (6:14)
58.   6 (6:15)
59.   3 (6:16)
60.   137 yrs (6:16)
61.   Amram (6:20)
62.   Amram and Jochebed (6:20)
63.   137 yrs (6:20)
64.   Elisheba (6:23)
65.   Nadab, Abhihu, Eleazar, Ithamar (6:23)
66.   Elisheba (6:23)
67.   Eleazar (6:25)
68.   Moses (7:1)
69.   Aaron (7:1)
70.   Moses – 80 yrs and Aaron – 83 yrs (7:7)
71.   Turning his walking stick into a snake (7:8-13)
72.   Hardened his heart (7:22-23)
73.   Egyptians (7:24)
74.   River Nile (7:14-24)
75.   Blood; Frogs; Gnats; Flies; Death of animals; Boils; Hail; Locusts; Darkness; Death of firstborn.
76.   The magicians of Egypt (8:19)
77.   Goshen (8:22)
78.   God (8:23)
79.   A handful of ashes (9:8-12)
80.   Boils (9:11)

81. Flax and Barley (9:31)
82. Wheat and Spelt (9:32)
83. Moses and Aaron (10:11)
84. A strong west wind (10:19)
85. Gulf of Suez (10:19)
86. For 3 days (10:22)
87. Pharaoh's face (10:27-29)
88. For gold and silver jewellery (11:2)
89. Moses (11:3)
90. Exodus 11:7
91. Passover (12:1)
92. On 10th day of the first month (12:3)
93. On the 14th day of the first month (12:6)
94. Bitter herbs and with bread made without yeast (12:8)
95. The Passover (12:11)
96. 7 days (12:18)
97. A sprig of hyssop (12:22)
98. The Israelites (12:34)
99. Sukkoth (12:37)
100. About 6,00,000 men (12:37)
101. For 430 yrs (12:40)
102. The Passover meal (12:43-44)
103. Passover (12:46)
104. Seven days
105. Abib (13:4)
106. The coast to Philistia (13:17)
107. If they saw war they might want to go back to Egypt (13:17-18)

108.   Joseph (13:19)
109.   Etham on the edge of the desert (13:20)
110.   Pillar of cloud during the day and pillar of fire during the night (13:21)
111.   In front of Pi Hahiroth (14:2)
112.   600 (14:7)
113.   The pillar of cloud (14:19-20)
114.   Strong wind (14:21)
115.   Israelites (14:22-29)
116.   Egyptians (14:25)
117.   Moab's (15:15)
118.   Miriam (15:20)
119.   Miriam (15:20)
120.   Miriam (15:20)
121.   Into the Sher Desert (15:22)
122.   Marah (15:23)
123.   At Marah (15:24)
124.   The water was bitter (15:22-24)
125.   A piece of wood (15:25)
126.   At Elim (15:27)
127.   Sin desert (16:1)
128.   Quails (16:13)
129.   Manna (16:13-36)
130.   2 kilo till 5 days and 4 kilo for the 6th and the 7th day (16:13-36)
131.   Israelites (16:31)
132.   2 kilo (16:33)
133.   40 years (16:35)

134. Rephidim (17:1)
135. Massah and Meribah (17:7)
136. Water from a rock (17:1-7)
137. At Rephidim (17:8)
138. Aaron and Hur (17:12)
139. The Lord is my Banner (17:15)
140. Amalekites (17:14)
141. Eliezer (18:3)
142. Jethro (18:13-26)
143. On the first day of the third month (19:1)
144. At the foot of Mount Sinai (19:2)
145. Kingdom of priests and a holy nation (19:5-6)
146. Mount Sinai (19:18)
147. To the 3rd and the 4th generations (20:5)
148. To the thousands of generations (20:6)
149. 6 (20:2-17)
150. Lightening, Thundering and Trumpet (20:18)
151. Out of stone which have no cuts (20:25)
152. 6 yrs (21:2)
153. When the slave doesn't want to be free (21:6)
154. To be put to death (21:15)
155. To be put to death (21:17)
156. He has to pay the amount which her husband demands with the approval of judges (21:22-25)
157. To be put to death (21:16)
158. It shall be stoned to death (21:28)
159. He was to be put to death (21:29)
160. The owner of the bull has to pay 30 pieces of silver to the owner of the slave (21:32)

161.   Death (22:19)

162.   By sunset (22:26)

163.   Bribe (23:8)

164.   Rest (23:12)

165.   3 times (23:14)

166.   Morning (23:18)

167.   Mother's milk (23:19)

168.   Miscarriage or barren women (23:26)

169.   Moses (24:4)

170.   Leaders of the Israelites (24:11)

171.   7th day (24:16)

172.   40 days (24:18)

173.   Moses (24:18)

174.   Acacia wood (25:10)

175.   2 ½ cubits long, 1 ½ cubit wide and 1 ½ cubit high (25:10)

176.   04 (25:12)

177.   2 ½ cubit long and 1 ½ cubit wide (25:17)

178.   2 cubits long, 1 cubit wide and 1 ½ cubit high (25:23)

179.   Sacred bread (25:30)

180.   Gold (25:31)

181.   A talent i.e. 75 pounds or about 34 kgs (25:39)

182.   10 (26:1)

183.   Linen, blue, purple and scarlet yarn (26:1)

184.   Goats' hair (26:7)

185.   10 cubits long and 1 ½ cubit wide (26:16)

186.   2 (26:17)

187.   48 {20+20+6+2} (26:18-23)

188.   15 {5+5+5} (26:26-27)

189. Curtain (26:33)
190. Altar (27:1-2)
191. 3 cubits high, 5 cubits long and 5 cubits wide (27:1-2)
192. Aaron and his sons (28:1)
193. Moses (28:2)
194. A breastplate, an ephod, a robe, a woven tunic, a turban and a sash (28:4)
195. Names of the children of Israel (28:21; 29)
196. Urim and Thummim {Revelation and Truth} (28:30)
197. Gold bells and pomegranates (28:34)
198. HOLY TO THE LORD (28:36)
199. Aaron (30:7)
200. Half shekel (30:12-14)
201. 20 (30:13)
202. Death (30:20-21)
203. Bezalel (31:2, 6)
204. Bezalel (31:2-3)
205. Uri (31:2)
206. Judah (31:2)
207. Dan (31:6)
208. Ahisamak (31:6)
209. Make us gods (32:1)
210. Levites (32:26)
211. Levites (32:28)
212. 3000 (32:28)
213. Face to face (33:11)
214. Moses (32:32)
215. Mount Horeb (33:6)

216. Tent of meeting (33:7)
217. Joshua (33:11)
218. Nun (33:11)
219. Moses (33:15)
220. Moses (33:18)
221. Moses (34:1-4)
222. Moses (34:27)
223. Moses (34:29)
224. Moses (34:30)
225. Moses (34:33)
226. Tabernacle
227. On the Sabbath day (35:3)
228. 29 talents and 730 shekels (38:24)
229. 100 talents and 1775 shekels (38:25)
230. 70 talents and 2400 shekels (38:29)
231. Memorial stones for the sons of Israel (39:6-7)
232. Breastplate (39:8-9)
233. The glory of the Lord filled the Tabernacle (40:34-35)
234. When the cloud lifted (40:36-37)

Who said to whom?
235. Jethro to his daughters (2:18)
236. Jethro to his daughters (2:20)
237. Jethro to his daughters (2:20)
238. Lord to Moses (3:5)
239. Lord to Moses (3:14)
240. Lord to Moses (4:2)
241. Lord to Moses (4:11)
242. Lord to Moses (4:12)

243. Moses to Lord (4:13)
244. Lord to Moses (4:14)
245. Lord to Moses (4:16)
246. Pharaoh to Moses and Aaron (5:4)
247. Pharaoh to Israelite overseers (5:17)
248. Israelite overseers to Moses and Aaron (5:21)
249. Moses to Lord (5:22)
250. Moses to Lord (6:12)
251. Moses to Pharaoh (8:10)
252. Pharaoh to Moses and Aaron (9:27)
253. Pharaoh to Moses and Aaron (9:28)
254. Pharaoh's official to Pharaoh (10:7)
255. Pharaoh's official to Pharaoh (10:7)
256. Pharaoh to Moses and Aaron (10:10)
257. Pharaoh to Moses and Aaron (10:16)
258. Pharaoh to Moses and Aaron (10:17)
259. Pharaoh to Moses (10:28)
260. Moses to Pharaoh (10:29)
261. Israelites to Moses (14:11)
262. Moses to the Israelites (14:13)
263. Moses to the Israelites (14:14)
264. Lord to Moses (14:15)
265. Jethro to Moses (18:17-18)
266. Jethro to Moses (18:18)
267. Jethro to Moses (18:19)
268. Jethro to Moses (18:22)
269. Israelites to Moses (20:19)
270. Moses to Israelites (32:30)

Answers – Exodus

271.   Moses to the Lord (33:13)
272.   Lord to Moses (33:20)
273.   Moses to the Lord (33:12)
274.   Lord to Moses (34:6)
275.   Moses to the Lord (34:9)
276.   Lord to Moses (34:11)
277.   Lord to Moses (34:12)

Leviticus

1.   27 chapters
2.   859 verses
3.   Moses
4.   1445-1444 B.C.
5.   5
6.   Burnt offering (1:3), Grain offering (2:2), Peace offering (7:12-31), Purification (Sin) offering (4:2-3), Guilt (Reparation) offering (5:16)
7.   Thanksgiving offering (7:12-15); Votive offering (7:16-17); Wave offering (7:30-31)
8.   Bullock, goat and pigeons (1:5; 10; 14)
9.   Aaron's sons (1:5; 11)
10.   Finest flour (2:1)
11.   Grain offering (2:2)
12.   Fine flour, oil and incense (2:2)
13.   Aaron and his sons (2:3)
14.   Yeast (2:11)
15.   Honey and yeast (2:11)
16.   Grain offering (2:13)
17.   Without any defect (3:1)
18.   2 doves or 2 young pigeons (5:7)
19.   Fellowship offering (3:6)
20.   A young bullock without any defect (4:1-12)
21.   A fifth part (5:15-16)
22.   The fire on the altar (6:8-13)
23.   It was broken (6:28)
24.   Peace offering (7:11-12)

25. Fellowship offering of thanksgiving (7:13)
26. 2 days (7:16)
27. Unclean person (7:20)
28. The priests (7:28-38)
29. 7 days (8:31-36)
30. Nadab and Abihu (10:1)
31. Nadab and Abihu (10:1-2)
32. Mishael and Elzaphan (10:4)
33. Uzziel (10:4)
34. Uzziel (10:4)
35. Strong drink (10:8-9)
36. Any animal that has a divided hoof and that chews the cud (11:3)
37. Camels, Hyrax (Rock-badgers) and Rabbit (11:4-6)
38. Pig (11:7)
39. Fins and scales (11:9-12)
40. 7 days (12:1-2)
41. 33 days (12:4)
42. 8th day (12:3)
43. 2 weeks (12:5)
44. 66 days (12:5)
45. Priest (13:38-39)
46. Torn clothes (13:45)
47. The person who is ceremonially clean of the infectious skin disease (14:8-9)
48. The priest (14:1-32)
49. The priest (14:39)
50. It was to be burned and torn down (14:44-45)
51. 2 goats (16:5)

52. Azazel (16:5-7)
53. Goat (16:10, 21-22)
54. Bull (16:11)
55. 7 times (16:14)
56. Once a year (16:33-34)
57. Blood (17:14)
58. Abomination (18:22)
59. Because the Lord our God is holy (19:1-2)
60. For the poor and foreigners (19:9-10)
61. Love your neighbor as yourself (19:18; Matt. 22:36-39)
62. You shall not make any cuttings in your flesh and you shall not print any marks on you (19:28)
63. 14th day of the 1st month (23:4-5)
64. Lord's festival of Unleavened Bread (23:6)
65. Festival of trumpets (23:24)
66. 10th day of the 7th month (23:27)
67. 15th day of the 7th month (23:34)
68. 7 days (23:34)
69. Shelomith (24:10-11)
70. Shelomith's son (24:10-12)
71. Every 50th year (25:8-17)
72. One year (25:29)
73. One of his kin (25:47-52)
74. 50 silver shekel (27:3)
75. 30 silver shekel (27:4)
76. 20 silver shekel (27:5)
77. 10 silver shekel (27:5)
78. 5 silver shekel for male and 3 silver shekel for female (27:6)

Answers – Leviticus

79. 15 silver shekel for male and 10 silver shekel for female (27:7)
80. 50 silver shekels (27:16)

Numbers

1. 36 chapters
2. 1288 verses
3. Moses
4. 1450-1410 B.C.
5. 20 years (1:3)
6. 603550 (1:1; 46)
7. Levites (1:47)
8. Levites (1:50)
9. Levites (1:53)
10. Nahshon (2:3)
11. Nethanel (2:5)
12. Eliab (2:7)
13. Judah (2:9)
14. Judah, Issachar and Zebulun (2:3-9)
15. Elizur (2:10)
16. Shelumiel (2:12)
17. Eliasaph (2:14)
18. Reuben, Simeon and Gad (2:10-16)
19. Elishama (2:18)
20. Gamaliel (2:20)
21. Abidan (2:22)
22. Ephraim, Manasseh and Benjamin (2:18-24)
23. Ahiezer (2:25)
24. Pagiel (2:27)
25. Ahira (2:29)
26. Dan, Asher and Naphtali (2:25-31)

27.   Nadab (3:2)
28.   Sinai Desert (3:4)
29.   Eleazer and Ithamar (3:4)
30.   Levi (3:17)
31.   7500 (3:22)
32.   Eliasaph (3:24)
33.   8600 (3:28)
34.   Kohathites (3:27-31)
35.   Elizaphan (3:30)
36.   Eleazer (3:32)
37.   6200 (3:34)
38.   Zuriel (3:35)
39.   East of the tabernacle (3:38)
40.   22000 (3:39)
41.   22273 (3:42-43)
42.   1365 shekels (3:50)
43.   Aaron and Moses (4:17)
44.   2750 (4:35)
45.   2630 (4:39-40)
46.   3200 (4:483-44)
47.   8580 (4:47-48)
48.   Water mixed with dust of the tabernacle floor (5:11-26)
49.   No razor come on his head (6:1-8)
50.   Aaron and his sons (6:23-26)
51.   Nahshon and Judah (7:12)
52.   130 shekels (7:85)
53.   70 shekels (7:85)

54.   2400 shekels (7:85)
55.   10 shekels (7:86)
56.   The voice of the Lord speaking to him (7:89)
57.   Levites (8:7)
58.   Levites (8:18)
59.   25-50 (8:24-25)
60.   Passover (9:4)
61.   Sinai Desert (9:5)
62.   A cloud (9:15)
63.   2 (10:2)
64.   The whole community (10:3)
65.   The leaders – the heads of the clans of Israel (10:4)
66.   The sons of Aaron (10:8)
67.   Judah (10:14-28)
68.   Hobab (10:29)
69.   "Rise up, Lord! May your enemies be scattered; may your foes flee before you." (10:35)
70.   "Return, Lord, to the countless thousands of Israel." (10:36)
71.   Taberah (11:1-3)
72.   It was like coriander seeds and looked like resin (11:7)
73.   When the dew fell in the night (11:9)
74.   Moses (11:12)
75.   70 (11:16-17)
76.   1 month (11:19-20)
77.   Eldad and Medad (11:26)
78.   Joshua (11:28)
79.   10 homers (11:32)
80.   A great plague (11:33-34)

Answers – Numbers

81. Kibroth Hattaavah (11:33-34)
82. Graves of cravings (11:34)
83. Moses (12:3)
84. Moses (12:7)
85. Moses (12:8)
86. Leprosy (12:9-14)
87. 7 days (12:14)
88. Hazeroth (12:16)
89. Desert of Paran (13:3)
90. Shammau (13:4)
91. Zaccur (13:4)
92. Shaphat (13:5)
93. Hori (13:5)
94. Jephunneh (13:6)
95. Judah (13:6)
96. Igal (13:7)
97. Joseph (13:7)
98. Nun (13:8)
99. Ephraim (13:8; 16)
100. Palti (13:9)
101. Raphu (13:9)
102. Gaddiel (13:10)
103. Sodi (13:10)
104. Gaddi (13:11)
105. Susi (13:11)
106. Ammiel (13:12)
107. Gemalli (13:12)
108. Sethur (13:13)

109. Michael (13:13)
110. Nahbi (13:14)
111. Vophsi (13:14)
112. Geuel (13:15)
113. Maki (13:15)
114. 12 (13:4-15)
115. Hosea (13:16)
116. Moses (13:16)
117. From the wilderness of Zin as far as Rehob (13:21)
118. Ahiman, Sheshai and Talmai (13:22)
119. 7 years (13:22)
120. Branch with grapes, pomegranates and figs (13:23)
121. Valley of Eshkol (13:24)
122. 40 days (13:25)
123. Caleb (13:30)
124. Desert of Paran (14:1; 13:3)
125. Desert of Paran (14:4; 13:3)
126. Joshua and Caleb (14:6)
127. Caleb and Joshua (14:6-9)
128. Israelites (14:22)
129. 20 (14:22-29)
130. 40 years (14:32-34)
131. Died by a plague (14:36-37)
132. Stoned to death (15:32-36)
133. Korah, Dathan, Abiram and On (16:1)
134. Eliab (16:1)
135. Levi (16:1)
136. 250 members (16:2)

137. Swallowed up by the earth (16:28-33)
138. 250 (16:35)
139. 12 (17:1-12)
140. 12 (17:7)
141. Aaron's (17:8)
142. To put the stick in front of the covenant box as a warning to the rebel Israelites (17:10)
143. Levites (18:20)
144. Lord Himself (18:20)
145. Levites (18:26)
146. A tenth part of the tithe (18:25-29)
147. A red heifer (19:1-10)
148. Kadesh (20:1)
149. He smote the rock (20:9-13)
150. Meribah (20:13)
151. Mount Hor (20:25-26)
152. 30 days (20:29)
153. Eleazar (20:22-29)
154. Hormah (21:3)
155. Destruction (21:3)
156. Bronze (21:9)
157. Looking on a brass serpent that Moses made and put on a pole (21:8-9)
158. Arnon River (21:13)
159. Arnon River (21:13)
160. Beer (21:16-18)
161. Heshbon (21:26)
162. Edrei (21:33)
163. Zippor (22:2)

164. Beor (22:5)
165. Balak (22:1-6)
166. Angel of the Lord (22:20-24)
167. 2 servants (22:22)
168. 3 times (22:28)
169. Balaam (22:29)
170. Bamoth Baal (22:41)
171. Balaam (23:10)
172. Balaam (23:10)
173. Zophim (23:14)
174. Israelites (23:23)
175. Balaam (23:23)
176. Balaam (24:10)
177. Balaam (24:16)
178. Balaam (24:17)
179. Amalek (24:20)
180. Shittim (25:1)
181. Phinehas (25:7-8)
182. 24000 (25:9)
183. Phinehas (25:11)
184. Phinehas (25:12)
185. Zimri (25:14)
186. Kozbi (25:15)
187. Zur (25:15)
188. Slightly less (26:1-51)
189. Er and Onan (26:19)
190. Mahlah, Noah, Hoglah, Milkah and Tirzah (26:33)
191. Serah (26:46)

192. Kohath (26:58)
193. Amram and Jochebed (26:59)
194. Miriam (26:59)
195. Makir (27:1)
196. Hepher (27:1)
197. Zelophehad's daughters (27:4-11)
198. Abarim mountain (27:12)
199. Joshua (27:15-18)
200. Wine offering which is also a food offering (28:1-8)
201. Her husband (30:6-8; 10-15)
202. 1000 men from each tribe (31:4)
203. Killed with the sword (31:8)
204. 32000 (31:34-35)
205. Caleb and Joshua (32:11-12)
206. Israelites (32:13)
207. Reuben, Gad and half the tribe of Manasseh (32:33)
208. Nebo and Baal Meon (32:37-38)
209. Clan of Machir (32:39)
210. Clan of Machir (32:40)
211. Nobah (32:42)
212. Kenath (32:42)
213. Kadesh (33:36)
214. Mount Hor (33:39)
215. 123 (33:39)
216. The Lord (34:1-12)
217. 48 (35:6-8)
218. 6 (35:6-15)
219. 3 (35:14)

220. 3 (35:14)
221. One who killed someone accidentally (35:22-25)
222. At least 2 witnesses (35:30)
223. The inheritance would remain in the tribe of the family of their father (36:1-12)

Who said to whom?
224. Moses to the people who became ceremonially unclean on account of a dead body (9:6-8)
225. Moses to Hobab (10:29)
226. Hobab to Moses (10:30)
227. Moses to Hobab (10:30)
228. Moses to Hobab (10:32)
229. Moses to the Lord (11:12)
230. Moses to the Lord (11:14)
231. Moses to the Lord (11:15)
232. Moses to Joshua (11:29)
233. Lord to Aaron and Miriam (12:6)
234. Aaron to Moses (12:11)
235. Joshua and Caleb to the Israelites (14:6-9)
236. Moses to the Lord (14:17)
237. Moses to Korah and his groups (16:5-9)
238. Moses and Aaron to the Lord (16:21-22)
239. Moabites to the elders of Midian (22:4)
240. Balak to Balaam (22:5)
241. Balak to Balaam (22:6)
242. Balak to Balaam (22:6)
243. Lord to Balaam (22:9)
244. Lord to Balaam (22:12)

245. Balaam to Balak's officials (22:13)
246. Balak to Balaam (22:17)
247. Balaam to donkey (22:29)
248. The angel of the Lord to Balaam (22:32)
249. The angel of the Lord to Balaam (22:32)
250. Balaam to the angel of the Lord (22:34)
251. Balak to Balaam (22:37)
252. Balaam to Balak (22:38)
253. Balaam to Balak (23:1)
254. Balaam to Balak (23:3)
255. Balaam to Balak (23:8)
256. Balak to Balaam (23:11)
257. Balaam to Balak (23:12)
258. Balaam to Balak (23:19)
259. Balaam to Balak (23:20)
260. Balak to Balaam (23:25)
261. Balaam to Balak (23:26)
262. Balak to Balaam (24:11)
263. Balak to Balaam (24:11)
264. Balaam to Balak (24:14)
265. Balaam to Balak (24:14)
266. Zelophehad's daughters to Moses (27:3)
267. Zelophehad's daughters to Moses (27:3)
268. Zelophehad's daughters to Moses (27:4)

Deuteronomy

1. 34 chapters
2. 959 verses
3. Moses
4. 1407-1406 B.C.
5. 11 days (1:2)
6. Sihon (1:3)
7. Ashtaroth (1:3)
8. Og (1:3)
9. Edrei (1:4)
10. River Euphrates (1:7)
11. Valley of Eshkol (1:24)
12. Because of their unbelief (1:32)
13. Caleb (1:36)
14. Encourage him (1:38)
15. Amorites (1:44)
16. Esau (2:5)
17. Edomites (2:6)
18. Lot and Esau (2:5, 9, 19)
19. Emites (2:10)
20. Emites (2:10-11)
21. Emites and Horites (2:10-12)
22. 38 years (2:14)
23. Zamzummites (2:20)
24. Desert of Kedemoth (2:26)
25. Argob (3:4)
26. Argob (3:4-5)

27. Sirion (3:9)
28. Senir (3:9)
29. Og (3:11)
30. 9 cubits long and 4 cubits wide (3:11)
31. Rabbah (3:11)
32. Region of Argob in Bashan (3:13)
33. Jair (3:14)
34. Dead Sea (3:17)
35. Mount Pisgah (3:27)
36. Add or take away any commandment (4:1-2)
37. Egypt (4:20)
38. They would be scattered among the nations (4:25-28)
39. Moses and the leaders of Israelite tribes (5:23)
40. The Lord our God is one God and love the Lord your God with all your heart, with all your soul and with all your might (6:4-5)
41. When they are discouraged (6:10:12)
42. Kill and destroy them completely (7:1-5)
43. Israelites (8:2)
44. 40 years (8:3)
45. Israelites (8:5)
46. Canaan (8:9)
47. To get wealth (8:17-18)
48. Anakites (9:2)
49. Ten Commandments (9:10)
50. Taberah, Massah and KibrothHattaavah (9:22)
51. Moses (9:25)
52. Moses (9:22-29)
53. In an ark of acacia wood (10:1-5)

54. Moserah (10:6)
55. Eleazer (10:6)
56. Levites (10:10)
57. Euphrates (11:24)
58. Stoned to death (13:6-11)
59. A chosen generation and a holy people to the Lord (14:1-2)
60. Turn it into money, go where the Lord chose, and buy food there (14:22-27)
61. Bring it for the Levites, strangers, fatherless and the widows to eat (14:28-29)
62. Lend to them but not borrow (15:6)
63. Pierce his ear (15:16-18)
64. Sacrifice it to the Lord (15:19-23)
65. To be like other nations (17:14-15)
66. Moses (18:15-19)
67. Their neighbors' landmark (19:14)
68. Two or three witnesses (19:15)
69. Peace offering (20:10-11)
70. Double (21:15-17)
71. Only that day (21:22-23)
72. Return it to the owner (22:1-4)
73. Bright red colors and clothing that pertained to the opposite sex (22:5, 11)
74. Ammonites and Moabites (23:3)
75. Pethor in Aram Naharaim (23:4)
76. Beor (23:4)
77. Dig a hole outside the camp, relieve yourself and then cover it (23:12-14)

78. Earnings of a male or female prostitute (23:18)
79. All the grapes they wanted but they could not put any in a vessel and ears of corn they could pluck with their hand; but they could not use a sickle (23:24-25)
80. 1 year (24:5)
81. Everyday (24:14-15)
82. 40 (25:1-3)
83. Blot out the remembrance of Amalekites (25:17-19)
84. Mount Ebal (27:4)
85. Mount Ebal (27:4)
86. Mount Gerizim (27:12)
87. Mount Ebal (27:13)
88. Simeon, Levi, Judah, Issachar, Joseph and Benjamin (27:12)
89. Reuben, Gad, Asher, Zebulun, Dan and Naphtali (27:13)
90. The priests (31:9-13)
91. Mount Nebo (32:49)
92. Abarim Range (32:49)
93. Gad (33:20)
94. Asher (33:24)
95. Jericho (34:3)
96. Moab (34:5)
97. In the valley opposite Beth Peor (34:6)
98. 120 years (34:7)
99. Moses (34:7)
100. In the plains of Moab (34:8)
101. 30 days (34:8)
102. Joshua (34:9)

Who said to whom?

103.   Israelites to Moses (1:14)

104.   Moses to Israelites (1:21)

105.   Israelites to Moses (1:41)

106.   Leaders of the tribes and the elders to Moses (5:24)

107.   Leaders of the tribes and the elders to Moses (5:25)

108.   Lord to Moses (5:28)

109.   Lord to Moses (5:30)

110.   Lord to Moses (5:31)

111.   Moses to the Israelites (6:4)

112.   Lord to Moses (9:12)

113.   Lord to Moses (9:13)

114.   Moses to the Israelites (9:24)

115.   Moses to Joshua (31:8)

116.   Moses to Levites (31:27)